Frederick
DOUGLASS
IN HIS OWN WORDS

Also by Milton Meltzer

Lincoln: In His Own Words

Thomas Jefferson: Revolutionary Aristocrat

George Washington and the Birth of Our Nation

Theodore Roosevelt and His America

Andrew Jackson and His America

Benjamin Franklin: The New American

Columbus and the World Around Him

Voices from the Civil War: A Documentary History of the Great American Conflict

The Black Americans: A History in Their Own Words

African American History: 400 Years of Black Life (with Langston Hughes)

The American Revolutionaries: A History in Their Own Words

The Bill of Rights: How We Got It and What It Means

Slavery: A World History

Cheap Raw Material: How Our Youngest Workers Are Exploited and Abused

Underground Man

Starting From Home: A Writer's Beginnings

Frederick
DOUGLASS
IN HIS OWN WORDS

EDITED BY

Milton Meltzer

ILLUSTRATED BY

Stephen Alcorn

HARCOURT BRACE & COMPANY

San Diego   New York   London

Requests for permission to make copies of any part of
the work should be mailed to: Permissions Department,
Harcourt Brace & Company, 6277 Sea Harbor Drive, Orlando,
Florida 32887-6777.

Library of Congress Cataloging-in-Publication Data
Douglass, Frederick, 1818–1895.
Frederick Douglass, in his own words/edited by Milton Meltzer;
illustrated by Stephen Alcorn.—1st ed.
p.   cm.
Includes bibliographical references and index.
ISBN 0-15-229492-9
1. Antislavery movements—United States.   2. Slavery—United States.
3. United States—Race relations.   4. United States—Social conditions—To 1865.
5. United States—Social conditions—1865–1918. 6. Douglass, Frederick, 1818–1895.
I. Meltzer, Milton, 1915–   . II. Title.
E449.D7324   1995
305.8'00973'09034—dc20   94-14524

Printed in Singapore

First edition
A B C D E

In memory of Langston Hughes
1902–1967
—M. M.

To Mother Africa, who with a sigh in her heart
was forced to fill the ships and watch her children depart
—S. A.

CONTENTS

CONTENTS

CONTENTS

BIOGRAPHICAL PROFILES AND PORTRAITS

AUTHOR'S NOTE

THE PAGES OF AFRICAN-AMERICAN HISTORY RICHLY DOCUMENT THE LIVES OF many distinguished men and women. Whatever period you turn to in the four-hundred-year span of that history, you will find the accounts of people who have not only endured much but accomplished much. Many have been singled out by biographers who have told their life stories and thus preserved a remarkable record for us.

Perhaps no figure from that past deserves more attention than Frederick Douglass. By common agreement of historians, he was the most renowned and influential black leader of the nineteenth century. His most recent biographer, William S. McFeely, called him "one of the giants of nineteenth-century America" who "stood as tall as any." John W. Blassingame, editor of *The Frederick Douglass Papers,* points out that "Douglass was not only a representative black man, he stood for what was best in American ideals." Douglass is remembered not only as one of the greatest orators of his day but as a writer of enduring cultural and literary significance.

Born a slave in Maryland in 1818, he escaped to freedom and by an iron will, hard work, and great talent helped to win his people's freedom. Douglass told his life story in three volumes of autobiography. The first, *Narrative of the Life of Frederick Douglass,* was published in 1845, when he was twenty-seven. The second, *My Bondage and My Freedom,* carried his story to 1855, when the book appeared. And the third, *The Life and Times of Frederick Douglass,* came out in 1881. (He died in 1895, at the age of seventy-seven.) These books are still in print in several editions.

Less than a year after his escape from bondage in 1838, Douglass began to speak at antislavery meetings in the North. Soon his eloquent indictment of slavery made him one of the most popular lecturers of the abolition movement in both the United States and Great Britain. In 1847 he began to publish his own weekly newspaper, the *North Star,* changing its name to *Frederick Doug-*

lass' Paper in 1851. In 1859 he launched his third periodical, *Frederick Douglass' Monthly*.

His speeches, articles, editorials, and letters not only give us many insights into the man himself and the thoughts and feelings of the African-American community, but they also help us to understand the attitudes of nineteenth-century America. "Perhaps better than any other nineteenth-century black American," wrote Waldo E. Martin Jr., "Douglass personified the travail and triumph of his people."

Douglass reached out to embrace almost every issue that concerned Americans troubled by injustice, inequality, and racism. He was, of course, a major figure among the abolitionists. But he also took part in many other reform movements—for women's rights, for labor, for temperance, against war and capital punishment, against lynching and peonage.

He was no plaster saint but a complex and contradictory man. He changed his mind and his public position on a number of crucial issues as time and experience taught him to see things from a different perspective.

For anyone who wants to trace in almost minute detail the twists and turns of social and political currents in the nineteenth century, study of the complete writings of Douglass is invaluable. But for others who do not have the time or the means to read all his work, a sampling of the thoughts of Douglass will be challenging and richly rewarding.

This book offers readers selections from the vast mass of Douglass's speeches and writings. The documents were chosen to represent his point of view on slavery, the struggle to overthrow it, the condition of free blacks both before and after Emancipation, the conduct of the Civil War and Lincoln's presidency, the era of Reconstruction, and the bleak years that came after it. Many of the major figures in that history are assessed by Douglass as he traces their actions and their impact.

No material is taken from the Douglass autobiographies, for they are readily available in most libraries and many bookstores. Some of the selections, however, do go into Douglass's personal history as he tells audiences or readers of his experiences in slavery and after. Some of the documents are given in full, but many have been shortened without changing their meaning. Paragraphing and punctuation have been modernized for the sake of easier reading.

ILLUSTRATOR'S NOTE

IN CREATING THE ART FOR THIS VOLUME OF FREDERICK DOUGLASS'S WRITINGS, I felt compelled to conceive of a series of images that, rather than literally illustrate specific passages of text, aim to provide the reader with a dramatic visual backdrop against which the epic tale of Frederick Douglass's life—as well as the trials and tribulations of generations of African-Americans—may unfold.

A visionary intent on raising the conscience of nineteenth-century America, Frederick Douglass possessed an extraordinary ability to transcend the constraints of his time. The breadth of his vision and imagination, which guided him on his long, arduous flight to freedom, enabled him to find the strength to lift the heavy burden thrust upon him at birth by that peculiar institution known as slavery.

Like Abraham Lincoln, Frederick Douglass was a man of his times, and like all great individuals, he did not develop in a vacuum. To emphasize just how much Frederick Douglass was shaped and affected by the forces surrounding him, I have included several portraits of Frederick Douglass's contemporaries.

Of the multitude of legendary anecdotes that the name Frederick Douglass brings to mind, one in particular came back, again and again, to haunt me as I prepared to work on this book. It relates to a time when, as a very young man, Frederick Douglass was forced to endure the unspeakable as his master made a brutal attempt to break his spirit. One can only imagine how the young Frederick Douglass, like countless others who suffered such atrocities, must have felt that fateful day as a dark, ominous cloud suddenly loomed over his world. That he should have survived such an ordeal with his spirit intact is extraordinary; that he went on to tell the world of his trials and triumphs with such eloquence offers one of the greatest legacies of the entire nineteenth century.

The irrepressible, dynamic thrust of the chain of events following that horrific experience made me realize that the images I was to create should be essentially rhythmic in nature. From the beginning I envisioned imagery that was both hypnotic and mysterious, imbued with textures and patterns bursting with energy, as if unwilling to conform to the boundaries of the very blocks I was to cut them on. This resulted in a cacophony of graphic invention kindred in spirit to that of a nineteenth-century crazy quilt.

Like a medieval scribe gone mad with design, I commenced to work on this cycle of prints, in search of a visual equivalent to that elusive, indomitable spirit that could not be broken.

BEFORE THE WAR

·⟨══════════════⟩·

SOMETIME IN FEBRUARY 1818, HARRIET BAILEY, A TWENTY-SIX-YEAR-OLD slave on Maryland's Eastern Shore, gave birth to her fourth child, Frederick Augustus Bailey. Frederick Douglass, as he later would call himself, saw very little of his mother. In his early years he lived with his grandmother, Betsy Bailey, in her cabin on the plantation. He did not know who his father was, except that he was a white man. His mother, almost a stranger to him, died when he was seven. His grandmother Betsy, whose husband was a free black woodcutter, was an expert in fishing and farming. The family worked on the Tuckahoe farm of Betsy's master, Aaron Anthony.

When Frederick was six, he was taken from his grandmother and placed at Wye House, an estate about a dozen miles away, near Chesapeake Bay. It was where Frederick's older brother Perry and his sisters Sarah and Eliza lived. Wye House was the center of the domain of Colonel Edward Lloyd, for whom Aaron Anthony worked. Lloyd was a former governor of Maryland and U.S. senator, whose immense lands and wealth were rooted in the slave labor system.

In 1818, the year of Frederick's birth, the population of the United States was just under ten million. Of these, 1.7 million were slaves and about 250,000 were free blacks. James Monroe, a Virginian, sat in the White House as the fifth president. There were twenty states in the young Union, half of them free states, half of them slave states. To the west lay territories soon to ask for admission to the Union. National expansion raised the question of what to do about slavery. The request of the Missouri Territory to enter the Union began a debate in Congress. Those opposed to the spread of slavery believed that no slavery should be allowed in any territory west of the Mississippi River. Congress, they said, had the power to keep slavery from spreading. Hadn't the Northwest Ordinance of 1787 outlawed slavery in the territory that later became the free states of Ohio, Indiana, Illinois, Michigan, and Wisconsin?

But Southerners in Congress argued that slaves were property, and property was protected by the Constitution. To ban slavery in the West would be to violate the Constitution. And of course, restricting slavery would limit the plantation system and ruin the South's economy.

After a long and heated debate, Congress adopted the Missouri Compromise of 1820. Missouri would come in as a slave state, with the parallel of 36°30' N as the boundary. North of that line, slavery would be prohibited—except in Missouri. South of that line, slavery would be permitted. At the same time, Maine was admitted as a free state, thus keeping the number of free and slave states equal. This balance, many thought, would prevent one section of the country from dominating the other.

But more farsighted leaders saw the compromise differently. Thomas Jefferson, now in old age, wrote that this so-called settlement filled him with terror for the future. He thought the end of the nation would come in the form of a civil war between the North and the South over slavery.

Frederick, just two years old, was fated to play a great role in the developing crisis.

I

What I Know of Slavery

At the age of eight, the slave Frederick Douglass was sent to live in Baltimore, in the home of Hugh and Sophia Auld. The boy welcomed the exciting life of the city, a major port and shipbuilding center. The streets of Baltimore were much less confining than life on a plantation. He worked first as a house servant and then as a shipyard laborer. He made friends among the free blacks who had built a community with their own churches and secular societies. Here he learned to read and write, helped by Sophia Auld, who was drawn to the lively, questioning mind of this slave child. But her husband put a quick stop to the crime, declaring that learning "would spoil the best nigger in the world . . . forever unfitting him for the duties of a slave."

The boy went on learning, teaching himself out of his only book, a Webster speller. Then, at twelve, with fifty cents he bought his own copy of The Columbian Orator. *It was both a collection of patriotic speeches and a handbook on oratory. In the book was a dialogue between a master and his slave, in which the master, makes the case for slavery while the slave eloquently justifies his right to rebel and run away. Here Frederick found the words for the thoughts he had not yet been able to articulate. He spoke aloud to himself the passionate appeals of the book's great orators, demanding liberty, calling for emancipation, urging men and women on to great futures. That one book made an enormous difference in his life.*

In the Baltimore shipyards, Douglass worked alongside free black caulkers. They formed a Mental Improvement Society to debate issues and stretch their minds. The only slave among them, Frederick learned what free life could be like and determined to escape. He helped other runaways escape and finally, on September 3, 1838, made his own successful break for freedom. He borrowed the identity card of a free black sailor, dressed himself as a sailor, and without incident traveled by train and ferry to New York. There he married Anna Murray, a free black he had met in Baltimore. Quakers sent the couple on to greater safety in New Bedford, Massachusetts.

A friend soon advised Frederick to change his name to make it more difficult for fugitive-slave hunters to track him down and return him to his master. The friend suggested he take the name of Douglas, a heroic character in Walter Scott's poem Lady of the Lake. *Adding another* s, *Frederick assumed a name he would make world-famous.*

To support his wife and growing family (they would have one daughter and three sons), Douglass got a job as a caulker in a boatyard. But when the white workers threatened to strike if this black man entered their trade, he was forced to take on all kinds of unskilled day-labor jobs. He joined Zion Chapel, a black Methodist congregation, where he met an abolitionist preacher who urged him to become a preacher, too. Twice he spoke up at chapel meetings to describe what slavery was like and why slaves should be set free. Once he heard William Lloyd Garrison deliver his powerful antislavery message to an integrated audience in Mechanics Hall. (Douglass was already a subscriber to Garrison's Liberator.) *That night he decided he would like to become an orator: slavery and its evils would be his subjects, and Garrison, his mentor.*

After hearing Douglass speak in church, a Quaker abolitionist asked him to

visit Nantucket Island so others could hear what he had to say. On the evening of August 16, 1841, Douglass made his first public address at a meeting of the Massachusetts Anti-Slavery Society. In the audience were Garrison and other movement leaders. His speech brought the audience cheering to its feet. It was the beginning of a great career in the movement. He was asked to become a salaried agent of the society. He would go out on the lecture circuit to tell the world what it was like to be a slave.

That fall Douglass moved his family to Lynn, a town near Boston. This is the record of one of his early speeches there.

I FEEL GREATLY EMBARRASSED WHEN I ATTEMPT TO ADDRESS AN AUDIENCE OF white people. I am not used to speaking to them, and it makes me tremble when I do so because I have always looked up to them with fear. My friends, I have come to tell you something about slavery—what I know of it, as I have felt it. When I came North, I was astonished to find that the abolitionists knew so much about it, that they were acquainted with its deadly effects as well as if they had lived in its midst. But though they give you its history— though they can depict its horrors—they cannot speak as I can from experience; they cannot refer you to a back covered with scars, as I can; for I have felt these wounds; I have suffered under the lash without the power of resisting. Yes, my blood has sprung out as the lash embedded itself in my flesh. And yet my master has the reputation of being a pious man and a good Christian. He was a class leader in the Methodist church. I have seen this pious class leader cross and tie the hands of one of his young female slaves and lash her on the bare skin and justify the deed by the quotation from the Bible, "He who knoweth his master's will and doeth it not, shall be beaten with many stripes."

Our masters do not hesitate to prove from the Bible that slavery is right, and ministers of the Gospel tell us that we were born to be slaves: to look at our hard hands and see how wisely Providence has adapted them to do the labor; and then tell us, holding up their delicate white hands, that theirs are not fit to work. Some of us know very well that we have not time to cease from labor, or ours would get soft, too; but I have heard the superstitious ones exclaim—and ignorant people are always superstitious—that "if ever a man told the truth, that one did."

A large portion of the slaves know that they have a right to their liberty. It is often talked about and read of, for some of us know how to read, although all our knowledge is gained in secret.

I well remember getting possession of a speech by John Quincy Adams, made in Congress about slavery and freedom, and reading it to my fellow slaves. Oh! What joy and gladness it produced to know that so great, so good a man was pleading for us, and further, to know that there was a large and growing class of people in the North called abolitionists, who were moving for our freedom. This is known all through the South, and cherished with gratitude. It has increased the slave's hope for liberty. Without it his heart would faint within him; his patience would be exhausted. On the agitation of this subject he has built his highest hopes. My friends, let it not be quieted, for upon you the slaves look for help. There will be no outbreaks, no insurrections, whilst you continue this excitement: let it cease, and the crimes that would follow cannot be told.

Emancipation, my friends, is that cure for slavery and its evils. It alone will give to the South peace and quietness. It will blot out the insults we have borne, will heal the wounds we have endured and are even now groaning under, will pacify the resentment which would kindle to a blaze were it not for your exertions, and, though it may never unite the many kindred and dear friends which slavery has torn asunder, it will be received with gratitude and a forgiving spirit. Ah! How the slave yearns for it; that he may be secure from the lash, that he may enjoy his family and no more be tortured with the worst feature of slavery—the separation of friends and families. The whip we can bear without a murmur, compared to the idea of separation. Oh, my friends, you cannot feel the slave's misery when he is separated from his kindred. The agony of the mother when parting from her children cannot be told. There is nothing we so much dread as to be sold farther south.

My friends, we are not taught from books; there is a law against teaching us, although I have heard some folks say we could not learn if we had a chance. The Northern people say so, but the South do not believe it, or they would not have laws with heavy penalties to prevent it. The Northern people think that if slavery were abolished we would all come North. They may be more afraid of the free colored people and the runaway slaves going South. We would all seek our home and our friends, but, more than all, to escape from Northern prejudice, would we go to the South. Prejudice against color is stronger North than South; it hangs around my neck like a heavy weight. It presses me out from among my fellow men, and, although I have met it at every step the three years I have been out of Southern slavery, I have been able, in spite of its influence, "to take good care of myself."

—*Pennsylvania Freeman,* October 20, 1841

2

PREJUDICE IN THE CHURCH

Douglass's triumph on Nantucket was followed by over five hundred speeches in the next five years. He sometimes spoke two or three times a day, week after week. Such lecture tours by black abolitionists challenged proslavery propaganda. It was impossible to listen to Frederick Douglass and believe in the myths of the contented slave and of the benevolence of masters. No white abolitionists, however gifted, could be as effective as the African-Americans. Their message was personal testimony. Douglass and the many other former slaves on the circuit undermined notions of black inferiority.

In this speech delivered in Plymouth, Massachusetts, in 1841, Douglass spoke of the prejudice he encountered in the church.

THERE WAS A GREAT REVIVAL OF RELIGION NOT LONG AGO—MANY WERE CONverted and "received" as they said, "into the kingdom of heaven." But it seems, the kingdom of heaven is like a net; at least so it was according to the practice of these pious Christians; and when the net was drawn ashore, they had to set down and cull out the fish. Well, it happened now that some of the fish had rather black scales; so these were sorted out and packed by themselves. But among those who experienced religion at this time was a colored girl; she was baptized in the same water as the rest, so she thought she might sit at the Lord's table and partake of the same sacramental elements with the others. The deacon handed round the cup, and when he came to the black girl, he could not pass her, for there was the minister looking right at him, and as he was a kind of abolitionist, the deacon was rather afraid of giving him offense, so he handed the girl the cup, and she tasted. Now it so happened that next to her sat a young lady who had been converted at the same time, baptized in the same water, and put her trust in the same blessed Savior; yet when the cup, containing the precious blood which had been shed for all, came to her, she rose in disdain and walked out of the church. Such was the religion she had experienced!

Another young lady fell into a trance. When she awoke, she declared she had been to heaven. Her friends were all anxious to know what and whom she had seen there, so she told the whole story. But there was one good old lady whose curiosity went beyond that of all the others—and she inquired of the girl that had the vision if she saw any black folks in heaven. After some hesitation, the reply was, "Oh! I didn't go into the kitchen!"

Thus you see, my hearers, this prejudice goes even into the church of God. And there are those who carry it so far that it is disagreeable to them even to think of going to heaven if colored people are going there, too. And whence comes it? The grand cause is slavery; but there are others less prominent: one of them is the way in which children in this part of the country are instructed to regard the blacks.

"Yes!" exclaimed an old gentleman, interrupting him, "when they behave wrong, they are told 'black man come catch you.' "

Yet people in general will say they like colored men as well as any other, but in their proper place! They assign us that place; they don't let us do it for ourselves nor will they allow us a voice in the decision. They will not allow that we have a head to think, and a heart to feel, and a soul to aspire. They treat us not as men but as dogs—they cry "Stu-boy!" and expect us to run and do their bidding. That's the way we are liked. You degrade us, and then ask why we are degraded—you shut our mouths, and then ask why we don't speak—you close your colleges and seminaries against us, and then ask why we don't know more.

But all this prejudice sinks into insignificance in my mind when compared with the enormous iniquity of the system which is its cause—the system that sold my four sisters and my brothers into bondage and which calls in its priests to defend it even from the Bible! The slaveholding ministers preach up the divine right of the slaveholders to property in their fellow men. The

Southern preachers say to the poor slave, "Oh! If you wish to be happy in time, happy in eternity, you must be obedient to your masters; their interest is yours. God made one portion of men to do the working and another to do the thinking; how good God is! Now you have no trouble or anxiety; but ah! you can't imagine how perplexing it is to your masters and mistresses to have so much thinking to do in your behalf! You cannot appreciate your blessings; you know not how happy a thing it is for you that you were born of that portion of the human family which has the working, instead of the thinking, to do! Oh! How grateful and obedient you ought to be to your masters! How beautiful are the arrangements of Providence! Look at your hard, horny hands—see how nicely they are adapted to the labor you have to perform! Look at our delicate fingers, so exactly fitted for our station, and see how manifest it is that God designed us to be His thinkers and you the workers—Oh! The wisdom of God!"

I used to attend a Methodist church in which my master was a class leader. He would talk most sanctimoniously about the dear Redeemer, who was sent "to preach deliverance to the captives and set at liberty them that are bruised"—he could pray at morning, pray at noon, and pray at night; yet he could lash up my poor cousin by his two thumbs and inflict stripes and blows upon his bare back till the blood streamed to the ground! All the time quoting scripture for his authority and appealing to that passage of the Holy Bible which says, "He that knoweth his master's will, and doeth it not, shall be beaten with many stripes!" Such was the amount of this good Methodist's piety.

—*National Anti-Slavery Standard*, December 23, 1841

3

SLAVERY HAS LANDED IN OUR MIDST

George Latimer was a fugitive slave whose Virginia master came to Boston in 1842 to claim him. Lawyers rose to the fugitive's defense, and abolitionists issued a special newspaper three times weekly to publicize the case. Judge Lemuel Shaw denied a jury trial to determine whether the runaway slave should be returned to his master. But Latimer's freedom was purchased with money raised by Garrison and Douglass.

As a result of the mass protest, Massachusetts adopted a law barring judges and law officers from acting to return fugitive slaves.

On November 8, 1842, Douglass wrote his first public letter defending Latimer and telling how it felt to be a fugitive. The Liberator *printed it.*

. . . SLAVERY, OUR ENEMY, HAS LANDED IN OUR VERY MIDST AND COMMENCED its bloody work. Just look at it; here is George Latimer—a man, a brother, a husband, a father—stamped with the likeness of the eternal God and redeemed by the blood of Jesus Christ, outlawed, hunted down like a wild beast, and ferociously dragged through the streets of Boston and incarcerated within the walls of Leverett Street jail. And all this is done in Boston— liberty-loving, slavery-hating Boston—intellectual, moral, and religious Boston. And why was this—what crime had George Latimer committed? He had committed the crime of availing himself of his natural rights, in defense of which the founders of this very Boston enveloped her in midnight darkness, with the smoke proceeding from their thundering artillery. What a horrible state of things is here presented. Boston has become the hunting ground of merciless man-hunters, and man-stealers.

Henceforth, we need not portray to the imagination of Northern people the flying slave making his way through thick and dark woods of the South, with white-fanged bloodhounds yelping on his bloodstained track, but refer to the streets of Boston, made dark and dense by crowds of professed Christians. Take a look at James B. Gray's new pack, turned loose on the track of poor Latimer. I see the bloodthirsty animals, smelling at every corner, part with each other, and meet again; they seem to be consulting as to the best mode of coming upon their victim. Now they look sad, discouraged; tired, they drag along, as if they were ashamed of their business and about to give up the chase; but presently they get a sight of their prey, their eyes brighten, they become more courageous, they approach their victim unlike the common hound. They come upon him softly, wagging their tails, pretending friendship, and do not pounce upon him until they have secured him beyond possible escape. Such is the character of James B. Gray's new pack of two-legged bloodhounds that hunted down George Latimer and dragged him away to the Leverett Street slave prison but a few days since.

We need not point to the sugar fields of Louisiana or to the rice swamps of Alabama for the bloody deeds of this soul-crushing system but to the city of the pilgrims. In future, we need not uncap the bloody cells of the horrible slave prisons of Norfolk, Richmond, Mobile, and New Orleans, and depict the wretched and forlorn condition of their miserable inmates, whose groans rend the air, pierce heaven, and disturb the Almighty; listen no longer at the snappings of the bloody slave-driver's lash. Withdraw your attention, for a moment, from the agonizing cries coming from hearts bursting with the keenest anguish at the South, gaze no longer upon the base, cold-blooded, heartless slave-dealer of the South, who lays his iron clutch upon the hearts of husband and wife and, with one mighty effort, tears the bleeding ligaments apart which before constituted the twain one flesh. I say, turn your attention from all this cruelty abroad, look now at home—follow me to your courts of justice— mark him who sits upon the bench. He may, or he may not—God grant he may not—tear George Latimer from a beloved wife and tender infant. But let us take a walk to the prison in which George Latimer is confined, inquire for the turnkey; let him open the large iron-barred door that leads you to the inner prison. You need go no farther. Hark! Listen! Hear the groans and cries of George Latimer, mingling with which may be heard the cry—my wife, my child—and all is still again.

. . . Men—husbands and fathers of Massachusetts—put yourselves in the place of George Latimer; feel his pain and anxiety of mind; give vent to the groans that are breaking through his fever-parched lips from a heart immersed in the deepest agony and suffering; rattle his chains; let his prospects be yours for the space of a few moments. Remember George Latimer in bonds as bound with him; keep in view the golden rule—"All things whatsoever ye would that men should do unto you, do ye even so to them. In as much as ye did it unto the least of these, my brethren, ye have done it unto me."

Now make up your minds to what your duty is to George Latimer, and when you have made your minds up, prepare to do it and take the consequences, and I have no fears of George Latimer going back. I can sympathize with George Latimer, having myself been cast into a miserable jail on suspicion of my intending to do what he is said to have done, viz., appropriating my own body to my use. . . .

—*The Liberator*, November 8, 1842

4

My Slave Experience in Maryland

In a speech at the twelfth annual convention of the American Anti-Slavery Society in New York on May 6, 1845, Douglass revealed for the first time some of the specific details of his years in slavery. It was, in a sense, a preview of his first autobiography, Narrative of the Life of Frederick Douglass: An American Slave, *to be published a few days later. He had begun writing the book in 1844, at the urging of Wendell Phillips and others. One motive for writing the book was to dispel in some people's minds the belief that he had never been a slave. "They said I did not talk like a slave, look like a slave, or act like a slave, and that they believed I had never been south of Mason and Dixon's line." By disclosing facts that could not have been known by anyone but a genuine fugitive, he would disprove the charge that he was an impostor.*

The book was meant to reach readers who had not heard him speak, as well as to confirm the impression of intellectual power made on his audiences. In those prewar decades, the Narrative *provided a stirring antislavery message. Now, over 150 years later, it has become a classic in autobiographical literature.*

I ran away from the South seven years ago—passing through this city in no little hurry, I assure you—and lived about three years in New Bedford, Massachusetts, before I became publicly known to the antislavery people. Since then I have been engaged for three years in telling the people what I know of it. I have come to this meeting to throw in my mite, and since no fugitive slave has preceded me, I am encouraged to say a word about the sunny South. I thought, when the eloquent female who addressed this audience a while ago was speaking of the horrors of slavery, that many an honest man would doubt the truth of the picture which she drew; and I can unite with the gentleman from Kentucky in saying that she came far short of describing them.

I can tell you what I have seen with my own eyes, felt on my own person, and know to have occurred in my own neighborhood. I am not from any of those states where the slaves are said to be in their most degraded condition, but from Maryland, where slavery is said to exist in its mildest form; yet I can stand here and relate atrocities which would make your blood to boil at the statement of them. I lived on the plantation of Colonel Lloyd, on the Eastern Shore of Maryland, and belonged to that gentleman's clerk. He owned, probably, not less than a thousand slaves.

I mention the name of this man, and also of the persons who perpetrated the deeds which I am about to relate, running the risk of being hurled back into interminable bondage—for I am yet a slave—yet for the sake of the cause, for the sake of humanity, I will mention the names and glory in running the risk. I have the gratification to know that if I fall by the utterance of truth in this matter, that if I shall be hurled back into bondage to gratify the slaveholder—to be killed by inches—that every drop of blood which I shall shed, every groan which I shall utter, every pain which shall rack my frame, every sob in which I shall indulge, shall be the instrument, under God, of tearing down the bloody pillar of slavery, and of hastening the day of deliverance for three million of my brethren in bondage.

I therefore tell the names of these bloody men, not because they are worse than other men would have been in their circumstances. No, they are bloody from necessity. Slavery makes it necessary for the slaveholder to commit all conceivable outrages upon the miserable slave. It is impossible to hold the slaves in bondage without this.

We had on the plantation an overseer by the name of Austin Gore, a man who was highly respected as an overseer—proud, ambitious, cruel, artful, obdurate. Nearly every slave stood in the utmost dread and horror of that man. His eye flashed confusion amongst them. He never spoke but to command, nor commanded but to be obeyed. He was lavish with the whip, sparing with his word. I have seen that man tie up men by the two hands and for two hours, at intervals, ply the lash. I have seen women stretched up on the limbs of trees and their bare backs made bloody with the lash. One slave refused to be whipped by him—I need not tell you that he was a man, though

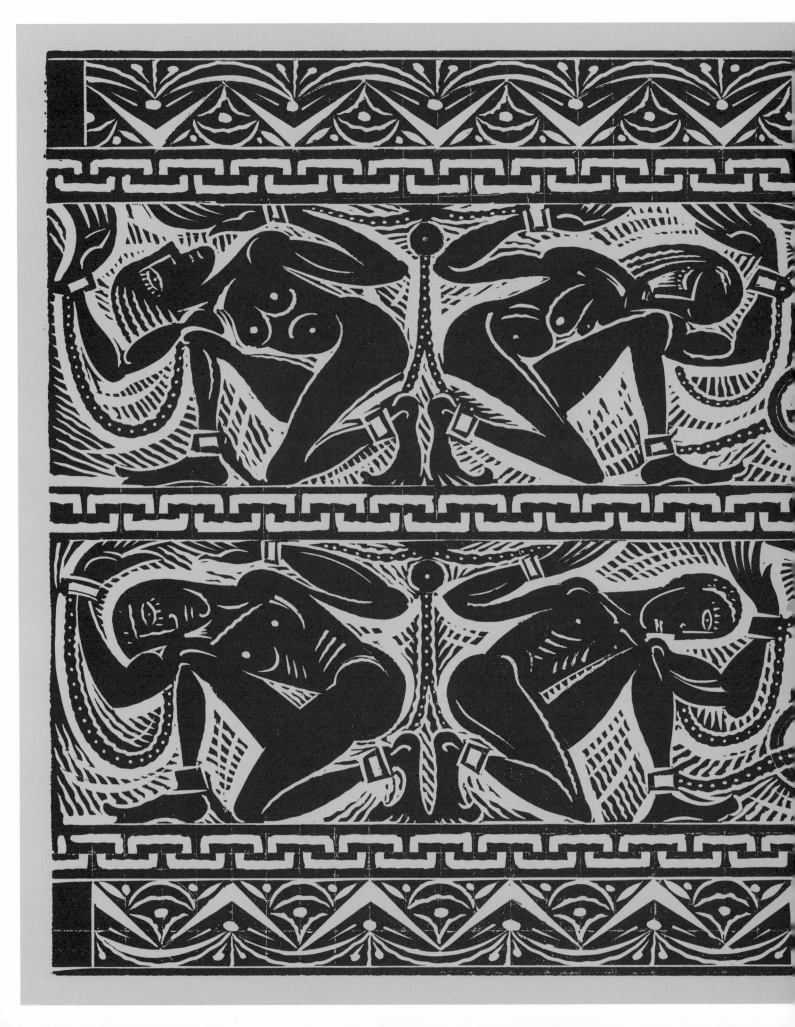

black his features, degraded his condition. He had committed some trifling offense—for they whip for trifling offenses. The slave refused to be whipped, and ran—he did not stand to and fight his master as I did once, and might do again, though I hope I shall not have occasion to do so—he ran and stood in a creek and refused to come out. At length his master told him he would shoot him if he did not come out. Three calls were to be given him. The first, second, and third were given, at each of which the slave stood his ground. Gore, equally determined and firm, raised his musket, and in an instant poor Derby was no more. He sank beneath the waves, and naught but the crimsoned waters marked the spot. Then a general outcry might be heard amongst us. Mr. Lloyd asked Gore why he had resorted to such a cruel measure. He replied, coolly, that he had done it from necessity: that the slave was setting a dangerous example and that if he was permitted to be corrected and yet save his life that the slaves would effectually rise and be freemen and their masters be slaves. His defense was satisfactory. He remained on the plantation, and his fame went abroad. He still lives in St. Michaels, Talbot County, Maryland, and is now, I presume, as much respected, as though his guilty soul had never been stained with his brother's blood.

I might go on and mention other facts if time would permit. My own wife had a dear cousin who was terribly mangled in her sleep, while nursing the child of a Mrs. Hicks. Finding the girl asleep, Mrs. Hicks beat her to death with a billet of wood, and the woman has never been brought to justice. It is not a crime to kill a Negro in Talbot County, Maryland, further than it is a deprivation of a man's property. I used to know of one who boasted that he had killed two slaves, and with an oath would say, "I'm the only benefactor in the country."

Now, my friends, pardon me for having detained you so long; but let me tell you with regard to the feelings of the slave. The people at the North say, "Why don't you rise? If we were thus treated we would rise and throw off the yoke. We would wade knee deep in blood before we would endure the bondage." You'd rise up! Who are these that are asking for manhood in the slave and who say that he has it not because he does not rise? The very men who are ready by the Constitution to bring the strength of the nation to put us down! You, the people of New York, the people of Massachusetts, of New England, of the whole Northern states, have sworn under God that we shall be slaves or die! And shall we three millions be taunted with a want of the love of freedom by the very men who stand upon us and say, submit or be crushed?

We don't ask you to engage in any physical warfare against the slaveholder. We only ask that in Massachusetts, and the several non-slaveholding states which maintain a union with the slaveholder—who stand with your heavy heels on the quivering heartstrings of the slave—that you will stand off. Leave us to take care of our masters. But here you come up to our masters and tell them that they ought to shoot us—to take away our wives and little ones— to sell our mothers into interminable bondage and sever the tenderest ties. You say to us, if you dare to carry out the principles of our fathers, we'll shoot you down. Others may tamely submit; not I. You may put the chains upon me and fetter me, but I am not a slave, for my master who puts the chains upon me shall stand in as much dread of me as I do of him. I ask you in the name of my three millions of brethren at the South. We know that we are unable to cope with you in numbers; you are numerically stronger, po- litically stronger, than we are—but we ask you if you will rend asunder the heart and [crush] the body of the slave? If so, you must do it at your own expense.

While you continue in the Union, you are as bad as the slaveholder. If you have thus wronged the poor black man by stripping him of his freedom, how are you going to give evidence of your repentance? Undo what you have done. Do you say that the slave ought not to be free? These hands— are they not mine? This body—is it not mine? Again, I am your brother, white as you are. I'm your blood-kin. You don't get rid of me so easily. I mean to hold on to you. And in this land of liberty, I'm a slave. The twenty- six states that blaze forth on your flag proclaim a compact to return me to bondage if I run away, and keep me in bondage if I submit. Wherever I go, under the aegis of your liberty, there I'm a slave. If I go to Lexington or Bunker Hill, there I'm a slave, chained in perpetual servitude. I may go to your deepest valley, to your highest mountain, I'm still a slave, and the bloodhound may chase me down.

Now I ask you if you are willing to have your country the hunting ground of the slave. God says thou shalt not oppress, the Constitution says oppress; which will you serve, God or man? The American Anti-Slavery Society says

God, and I am thankful for it. In the name of my brethren, to you, Mr. President, and the noble band who cluster around you, to you, who are scouted on every hand by priest, people, politician, church, and state, to you I bring a thankful heart, and in the name of three millions of slaves, I offer you their gratitude for your faithful advocacy in behalf of the slave.

—*National Anti-Slavery Standard*, May 22, 1845

5

WHAT THEY PRETEND

Almost everywhere Douglass went, he experienced discrimination. Professor John Blassingame, a close student of his lecture tours, noted that "stagecoach drivers, ship captains, and railroad conductors tried to separate him from white passengers; innkeepers and hotel owners denied him rooms; restaurant owners tried to force him to eat at a table set apart from those of whites. Douglass resisted these efforts, suing transportation companies, refusing to leave hotels and restaurants, and rejecting segregated seating arrangements for his audiences." He constantly challenged white racism, pointing out the illogic of its arguments and the hollowness of its rationalizations. In an article written for an antislavery publication, Douglass takes on people like Dr. Dewey, an American traveling abroad, who tried to defend slavery and discrimination before foreign audiences.

WHEN THEY TELL THE WORLD THAT THE NEGRO IS IGNORANT, AND NATURALLY and intellectually incapacitated to appreciate and enjoy freedom, they also publish their own condemnation by bringing to light those infamous laws by which the slave is compelled to live in the grossest ignorance. When they tell the world that the slave is immoral, vicious, and degraded, they but invite attention to their own depravity: for the world sees the slave stripped by his accusers of every safeguard to virtue, even of that purest and most sacred institution of marriage. When they represent the slave as being destitute of religious principle—as in the preceding cases—they profit nothing by the plea. In addition to their moral condemnation they brand themselves with bold and daring impiety in making it an offense punishable with fine and imprisonment, and even death, to teach a slave to read the will of God. When they pretend that they hold the slave out of actual regard to the slave's welfare, and not because of any profit which accrues to themselves as owners, they are covered with confusion by the single fact that Virginia alone has realized, in one short year, eighteen millions of dollars from the sale of human flesh. When they attempt to shield themselves by the grossly absurd and wicked pretense that the slave is contented and happy, and, therefore, "better off" in slavery than he could be possessed of freedom, their shield is broken by that long and bloody list of advertisements for runaway slaves who have left their happy homes and sought for freedom, even at the hazard of losing their lives in the attempt to gain it. When it is most foolishly asserted by Henry Clay, and those he represents, that the freedom of the colored is incompatible with the liberty of the white people of this country, the wicked intent of its author and the barefaced absurdity of the proposition are equally manifest. And when John C. Calhoun and Senator Walker attempt to prove that freedom is fraught with deafness, insanity, and blindness to the people of color, their whole refuge of lies is swept away by the palpable inaccuracy of the last United States census. And when, to cap the climax, Dr. Dewey tells the people of England that the white and colored people in this country are separated by an "impassable barrier," the hundreds of thousands of mulattoes, quadroons, etc., in this country silently but unequivocally brand him with the guilt of having uttered a most egregious falsehood. . . .

—*The Liberty Bell,* 1845

6

FOR GOD'S SAKE, A PENNY TO BUY SOME BREAD?

Priced at fifty cents, the 125-page Narrative *proved enormously popular. It sold about thirty thousand copies in the United States and Europe and was translated into French and German. It stopped rumors about Douglass's authenticity as a slave, but abolitionists feared its details might put slavecatchers on his trail. So Douglass set off for Great Britain, partly to avoid recapture and partly to advance the cause of antislavery among its many friends abroad. He was not the first ex-slave to speak to foreign audiences, but his reputation drew great crowds to see and hear him. He would be gone nearly two years, lecturing in England, Scotland, and Ireland.*

The British gave solid testimony of how highly they esteemed Douglass. In the fall of 1846 the abolitionists raised the funds to buy Douglass's freedom from Hugh Auld. And before he left for home, they raised $2,175 for Douglass to purchase a printing press needed to issue his own newspaper in the States.

Visiting Ireland, Douglass saw the appalling devastation caused by the potato famine, which had begun in the summer of 1845. Although deeply involved in seeking the overthrow of the slave system, he was not insensitive "to other evils that afflict and blast the happiness of mankind." In a letter home to Garrison's newspaper, he tells what he saw.

. . . THOUGH I AM MORE CLOSELY CONNECTED AND IDENTIFIED WITH ONE CLASS of outraged, oppressed, and enslaved people, I cannot allow myself to be insensible to the wrongs and sufferings of any part of the great family of man. I am not only an American slave but a man, and as such, am bound to use my powers for the welfare of the whole human brotherhood. . . . I had heard much of the misery and wretchedness of the Irish people, previous to leaving the United States, and was prepared to witness much on my arrival in Ireland. But I must confess, my experience has convinced me that the half has not been told. . . .

I spent nearly six weeks in Dublin, and the scenes I there witnessed were such as to make me "blush and hang my head to think myself a man." I speak truly when I say I dreaded to go out of the house. The streets were almost literally alive with beggars displaying the greatest wretchedness; some of them mere stumps of men—without feet, without legs, without hands, without arms—and others still more horribly deformed, with crooked limbs, down upon their hands and knees, their feet lapped around each other, and laid upon their backs, pressing their way through the muddy streets and merciless crowd, casting sad looks to the right and left in the hope of catching the eye of a passing stranger—the citizens generally having set their faces against giving to beggars. I have had more than a dozen around me at one time—men, women, and children—all telling a tale of woe which would move any but a heart of iron. Women, barefooted and bareheaded, and only covered by rags which seemed to be held together by the very dirt and filth with which they were covered—many of these had infants in their arms, whose emaciated forms, sunken eyes, and pallid cheeks told too plainly that they had nursed till they had nursed in vain. . . .

The spectacle that affected me most, and made the most vivid impression on my mind of the extreme poverty and wretchedness of the poor of Dublin, was the frequency with which I met little children in the street at a late hour of the night, covered with filthy rags and seated upon cold stone steps or in corners, leaning against brick walls, fast asleep, with none to look upon them, none to care for them. If they have parents, they have become vicious and have abandoned them. Poor creatures! They are left without help to find their way through a frowning world—a world that seems to regard them as intruders and to be punished as such. God help the poor!

. . . During my stay in Dublin, I took occasion to visit the huts of the poor in its vicinity—and of all places to witness human misery, ignorance, degradation, filth, and wretchedness, an Irish hut is preeminent. It seems to be constructed to promote the very reverse of everything like domestic comfort. If I were to describe one, it would appear about as follows: Four mud walls about six feet high, occupying a space of ground about ten feet square, covered or thatched with straw; a mud chimney at one end, reaching about a foot above the roof; without apartments or divisions of any kind; without floor, without windows, and sometimes without a chimney; a piece of pine board laid on the top of a box or an old chest; a pile of straw covered with dirty garments, which it would puzzle any one to determine the original part of any of them; a picture representing the crucifixion of Christ pasted on the most conspicuous place on the wall; a few broken dishes stuck up in a corner; an iron pot, or the half of an iron pot, in one corner of the chimney; a little peat in the fireplace, aggravating one occasionally with a glimpse of fire but sending out very little heat; a man and his wife and five children, and a pig. . . .

He who really and truly feels for the American slave cannot steel his heart to the woes of others; and he who thinks himself an abolitionist, yet cannot enter into the wrongs of others, has yet to find a true foundation for his antislavery faith. . . .

—*The Liberator*, March 27, 1846

7

A HOWLING MOB

No matter how logical, clear, and forceful a speech might be, not every audience was receptive to it. An abolitionist orator needed "strong nerves, a determined will, and moral course," Douglass said. He believed the human voice, more than the printed word, was the most effective tool. Yet face-to-face confrontation with an audience could be tumultuous and end in defeat. In some towns no hall was open to antislavery speakers. They might be forced to go out on the streets to ask people to listen to what they had to say.

After one such attempt to hold a meeting in Harrisburg, Pennsylvania, Douglass wrote this letter, describing mob law, to Sydney Howard Gay, an editor of the National Anti-Slavery Standard.

. . . A MEETING WAS CONVENED IN THE COURTHOUSE OF THIS TOWN LAST NIGHT to hear addresses on slavery by Mr. Garrison and myself. At the time appointed, Mr. Garrison was present and commenced the meeting by a calm statement of facts respecting the character of slavery and the slave power, showing in how many ways it was a matter deeply affecting the rights and interests of the Northern people. He spoke with little or no interruption for the space of an hour and then introduced me to the audience. I spoke only for a few moments when through the windows was poured a volley of unmerchantable eggs, scattering the contents on the desk at which I stood and upon the wall behind me and filling the room with the most disgusting and stifling stench. The audience appeared alarmed, but disposed to stay, though greatly at the expense of their olfactory nerves.

I, thinking I could stand it as well as my audience, proceeded with my speech, but in a very few moments we were interrupted and startled by the explosion of a pack of crackers, which kept up a noise for about a minute similar to the discharge of pistols, and being on the ladies' side, created much excitement and alarm. When this subsided, I again proceeded, but was at once interrupted again by another volley of addled eggs, which again scented the house with slavery's choice incense. Cayenne pepper and Scotch snuff were freely used and produced their natural results among the audience.

I proceeded again and was again interrupted by another grand influx of rotten eggs. One struck friend Garrison on the back, sprinkling its essence all over his honored head. At this point a general tumult ensued, the people in the house became much disturbed and alarmed, and there was a press toward the doorway, which was completely wedged with people. The mob was now howling with fiendish rage. I could occasionally hear amid the tumult, fierce and bloody cries, "Throw out the n——r, THROW OUT THE N——R." Here friend Garrison rose, with that calm and tranquil dignity altogether peculiar to himself, and said—speaking for himself and me—Our mission to Harrisburg is ended. If there be not sufficient love of liberty, and self-respect in this place, to protect the right of assembling and the freedom of speech, he would not degrade himself by attempting to speak under such circumstances, and he would therefore recall the appointment for Sunday night and go where he could be heard.

—*National Anti-Slavery Standard*, August 19, 1847

8

IN ALL TIMES, ALL NATIONS

West Indies Emancipation Day, August 1, 1833, was celebrated every year by African-American abolitionists. In 1847, Douglass gave the principal address on August 1, at Canandaigua, New York. He called the day the "glorious" anniversary of "the greatest, grandest" event of the nineteenth century. However, to grasp how important was Britain's freeing of the slaves in her West Indies colonies, the public needs to understand the greatness of the evil it ended and the centuries of labor that went into bringing it about. He then sketched in for his audience the history of slavery.

. . . FROM THE EARLIEST PERIODS OF MAN'S HISTORY, WE ARE ABLE TO TRACE manifestations of that spirit of selfishness which leads one man to prey upon the rights and interests of his fellow men. Love of ease, love of power, a strong human heart. These elements of character, overriding all the better promptings of human nature, have cursed the world with slavery and kindred crimes. Weakness has ever been the prey of power, and ignorance of intelligence. Joseph was sold into Egyptian bondage by his own brethren at a time when he ought to have been most dear unto them. The famine-stricken Israelites were reduced to bondage, when their sufferings ought to have aroused the most benevolent energies of the human heart. The Helots were consigned to serfdom or slavery, while yet smarting under wounds received in battle for their country. The proud Anglo-Saxons, overpowered in war, had their property confiscated by their haughty Norman superiors and were enslaved upon their own sacred soil. There are, at this moment, not fewer than forty million white slaves in Russia, a number far exceeding the present number of black slaves.

However much we may deplore the wickedness of such wholesale slavery, it is somewhat consoling that all nations have had a share of it, and that it cannot be said to be the peculiar condition of our race, any more than others. "He that leadeth into captivity, shall go into captivity," is a truth confirmed by all history and will remain immutably true.

Who were the fathers of our present haughty oppressors in this land? They were, until within the last four centuries, the miserable slaves, the degraded serfs, of Norman nobles. They were subjected to every species of brutality which their fiendish oppressors could invent. They were regarded as an inferior race—unfit to be trusted with their own rights. They were not even allowed to walk on the public highway and travel from town without written permission from their owners. They could not hold any property whatever but were themselves property, bought and sold. They were not permitted to give testimony in courts of law. They were punished for crimes, which, if committed by their haughty masters, were not deemed worthy of punishment at all. They were not allowed to marry without the consent of their owners. They were subjected to the lash and might even be murdered with impunity by their cruel masters. But, Sir, I must not dwell here, though a profitable comparison might be drawn between the condition of the colored slaves of our land and the ancient Anglo-Saxon slaves of England.

I come at once to the history of the enslavement of that race, whose deliverance from thralldom we have met to celebrate. The Slave Trade, by which slavery was introduced and established in the British West Indies, was commenced in the reign of Elizabeth, 1562. Spain and Italy had long been

engaged in the traffic, and England, no doubt tempted by their success, was induced, reluctantly, to follow in their footsteps. I say reluctantly, because from the first, the great princess, Elizabeth, seems to have entertained religious scruples concerning it and to have revolted at the thought of it. This is inferred from a conversation which the Queen had with Sir John Hawkins, on his return from his first slave-trading voyage. At this interview, she expressed her concern lest any of the Africans should be carried off without their consent, declaring it would be detestable and would call down the vengeance of heaven upon the undertakers! This pious outburst, though monstrous and absurd as coming from one who had just given her royal assent to this infernal traffic, was the natural result of her wicked position and is not without its parallel in our land. It was like Pilate delivering the Lamb of Calvary to the iron-hearted murderers, and washing his hands of his blood. Of course, the declarations of the Queen were disregarded. It could not be otherwise. To make merchandise of man, and treat him kindly and respect his will is morally impossible. The expression of the queen, if sincere, may be creditable to her humanity, but it is a dark reflection on her sagacity. The will of a victim is never respected. The lamb committed to the wolf may expect no quarter. The injustice, cruelty, and barbarity of this unhuman traffic can never be told or conceived. They are known only to God. He alone can fully comprehend them. We mortal and finite beings can only receive a partial view of them.

To assist in this, let us imagine what must be far less than the whole truth. Let us go to that little village on the West Coast of Africa. The inhabitants are quiet, simple, peaceful, and happy. It is evening. Through the rents and crevices of their fragile dwellings, a bright moon pours her soft and tranquil rays. The day's work is done, and the profound stillness is only relieved by the melodious hum of tropical insects. How sweet the scene. The husband and wife, the parent and child, the sister and brother, and "friends of the kindred tie," have met to while away the evening hour in simple talk and innocent song, and how sweet the moments glide. At the hour appointed, the mother clasps her innocent babe to her bosom, and with looks and words of love and admonition, she retires. Soon all follow, and our hut and village is still. The unsuspecting inhabitants are in the arms of "Nature's soft nurse," "and lulled with sounds of sweetest melody." They sleep on the brink of destruction.

Let us leave for a moment this happy village and go to the shore. A slave ship is anchored off the coast. On her deck, dim lights are seen in motion. A boat is now lowered from the side, and softly rowed ashore. Twelve armed men land. Their swords, guns, and cutlasses reflect the moonlight. When ready for their infernal work, they move off stealthily toward the doomed village. They are met by some wretch calling himself a prince, who, bribed by this wicked crew, becomes the treacherous instrument of destruction to this abode of happiness and the enslavement of its unoffending people. A few moments, and the village is in flames. The fear-smitten people start forth from the devouring fire, and in the hour of surprise and consternation, its people have become the prey of the spoiler. Grim death and desolation reigns, where before was life, peace, and joy.

Let us follow those despoiled people a short distance on their voyage to West Indian bondage. Chained and handcuffed, they are driven before cutlasses and pistols to the ship. Their path is marked with blood. Torn from home, despoiled of their freedom, they go to drag out a miserable existence in colonial slavery. What pain, what anguish, what agony of soul struggles beneath the hatchway of that pirate ship. They are stowed away, with as little regard to health as to decency. Breathing the putrid air inseparable from being so closely packed, disease and death soon reign in their infernal dungeon. Many of them become food for the hungry shark, who reddens the wake of a slave ship with their blood. And by the time they land at their point of destination, one-third of all taken on board have been thrown overboard during the voyage, and more horrible still, many have been thrown overboard alive, lest they should spread the death-dealing contagion among the rest. Those who reach the shore are sick, emaciated, and covered with sores. Landed on English soil, strangers to the English tongue, their only language is that of the lash. Before the bloody lash they are driven to market, and under the cry of the auctioneer, they are sold and separated from each other. All is lost! They are they know not where. Such is but a faint picture of that trade, which is even now plied, and which peopled with slaves the Western Isles and made Liverpool, Glasgow, and Bristol rich on the blood, bones, and sinews of men. A view of this God-defying trade led the great anti-slavery poet of England to cry out in the agony of his mighty soul:

> Is there not some chosen curse,
>   Hid in the stores of Heaven,
>   red with uncommon wrath,
> To blast the man, who gains his fortune
>   By the blood of souls.
>   —*National Anti-Slavery Standard*, August 19, 1847

9

THESE INFERNAL LAWS

While lecturing in Ohio with William Lloyd Garrison, Douglass observed the destructive effects of the so-called "black laws" upon the African-Americans of that state. He describes how they restricted the liberties and activities of the free blacks, reducing them almost to the condition of slavery. In this letter to Sydney Howard Gay he urges a campaign for their repeal.

. . . YOU ARE AWARE THAT WHAT ARE CALLED THE BLACK LAWS OF THIS STATE disallow and prohibit the testimony of colored persons against white persons in courts of law. By this diabolical arrangement, law, as a means of protecting the property and persons of the weak, becomes meaningless, since it gives a "thug" commission to any and every white villain and permits them to insult, cheat, and plunder colored persons with the utmost impunity. A score of facts might be mentioned of cases where persons having the fortune to have a white skin, have, in the presence of colored persons, taken away their property without remuneration, and the guilty persons could not be brought to condign punishment because their victims were black.

These shameful laws are not the natural expression of the moral sentiment of Ohio but the servile work of pandering politicians, who, to conciliate the favor of slaveholders and win their way into political power, have enacted these infernal laws. Let the people of Ohio demand their instant repeal and the complete enfranchisement of her colored people, and their gallant state would speedily become the paragon of all the free states, securing the gratitude and love of her colored citizens and wiping out a most foul imputation from the character of her white citizens. She might then well boast that justice within her borders, like its author in heaven, is without respect to persons. . . .

—*National Anti-Slavery Standard*, September 23, 1847

10

OUR MIND IS MADE UP

In November 1847, Douglass moved his family from Lynn, Massachusetts, to Rochester, New York. He was at the same time breaking free of Garrison's influence and, against his mentor's objections, launching his own newspaper, the North Star. *He wanted to fight for abolition in his own way, to reach readers with his own words, his own understanding of the shifting necessities of the antislavery movement. He had come back from England seven months earlier with a powerful desire to be independent and with the funds to realize his ambition as editor.*

Resenting his departure, and perhaps his rapidly growing celebrity, the Garrison people dropped him as lecturer. But Douglass did not feel stranded. He would be both editor and lecturer, ending his antislavery meetings with a call for new subscribers. Out on the lecture circuit he would gather news and develop editorial positions to advance abolition. He found continued support from his British friends and a strong backer in a wealthy white upstate New Yorker, Gerrit Smith. A generous philanthropist and abolitionist, Smith owned vast tracts of land and gave grants of forty acres each to Douglass and other black leaders he hoped would settle upstate.

In the first issue of the North Star, *Douglass told why blacks could and should be in the vanguard of the journalistic campaign against slavery.*

. . . IT IS NEITHER A REFLECTION ON THE FIDELITY NOR A DISPARAGEMENT OF the ability of our friends and fellow laborers to assert what "common sense affirms and only folly denies," that the man who has suffered the wrong is

the man to demand redress—that the man struck is the man to cry out—and that he who has endured the cruel pangs of slavery is the man to advocate liberty. It is evident we must be our own representatives and advocates, not exclusively but peculiarly—not distinct from but in connection with our white friends. In the grand struggle for liberty and equality now waging, it is meet, right, and essential that there should arise in our ranks authors and editors, as well as orators, for it is in these capacities that the most permanent good can be rendered to our cause.

Hitherto the immediate victims of slavery and prejudice, owing to various causes, have had little share in this department of effort: they have frequently undertaken and almost as frequently failed. This latter fact has often been urged by our friends against our engaging in the present enterprise; but, so far from convincing us of the impolicy of our course, it serves to confirm us in the necessity, if not the wisdom, of our undertaking. That others have failed is a reason for our earnestly endeavoring to succeed. Our race must be vindicated from the embarrassing imputations resulting from former nonsuccess. We believe that what ought to be done can be done. We say this in no self-confident or boastful spirit, but with a full sense of our weakness and unworthiness, relying upon the Most High for wisdom and strength to support us in our righteous undertaking. We are not wholly unaware of the duties, hardships, and responsibilities of our position. We have easily imagined some, and friends have not hesitated to inform us of others. Many doubtless are yet to be revealed by that infallible teacher, experience. A view of them solemnize but do not appall us. We have counted the cost. Our mind is made up, and we are resolved to go forward.

—*North Star*, December 3, 1847

11

A DISGRACEFUL AND CRUEL WAR

The war with Mexico, which had gone on for nearly two years, was within a week of ending when Douglass wrote this furious attack upon the American politicians who had failed to stop it. Through the treaty that ended the war, the United

States gained vast territories from Mexico. Would the new lands be organized into free or slave states? The issue of slavery would break apart both major parties and dominate politics in the decade that lay ahead.

FROM AUGHT THAT APPEARS IN THE PRESENT POSITION AND MOVEMENTS OF THE executive and cabinet, the proceedings of either branch of the national Congress, the several state legislatures, North and South, the spirit of the public press, the conduct of leading men, and the general views and feelings of the people of the United States at large, slight hope can rationally be predicted of a very speedy termination of the present disgraceful, cruel, and iniquitous war with our sister republic.

Mexico seems a doomed victim to Anglo-Saxon cupidity and love of domination. The determination of our slaveholding president to prosecute the war, and the probability of his success in wringing from the people men and money to carry it on, is made evident, rather than doubtful, by the puny opposition arrayed against him. No politician of any considerable distinction or eminence seems willing to hazard his popularity with his party, or stem the fierce current of executive influence, by an open and unqualified disapprobation of the war. None seem willing to take their stand for peace at all risks; and all seem willing that the war should be carried on, in some form or other.

If any oppose the president's demands, it is not because they hate the war but for want of information as to the aims and objects of the war. The boldest declaration on this point is that of Honorable John P. Hale, which is to the effect that he will not vote a single dollar to the president for carrying on the war. Mr. Hale knows, as well as the president can inform him, for what the war is waged; and yet he accompanies his declaration with that prudent proviso. This shows how deep-seated and strongly bulwarked is the evil against which we contend. The boldest dare not fully grapple with it.

Meanwhile, "the plot thickens"; the evil spreads. Large demands are made on the national treasury. (To wit: the poor man's pockets.) Eloquent and patriotic speeches are made in the Senate, House of Representatives, and state assemblies. Whig as well as Democratic governors stand stoutly up for the war; experienced and hoary-headed statesmen tax their declining strength and ingenuity in devising ways and means for advancing the infernal work, recruiting sergeants and corporals to perambulate the land in search of victims for the sword and food for powder. Wherever there is a sink of iniquity, or a den of pollution, these buzzards may be found in search of their filthy prey. They dive into the rum shop, and gambling house, and other sinks too infamous to name, with swinelike avidity, in pursuit of degraded men to vindicate the insulted honor of our Christian country.

Military chieftains and heroes multiply, and towering high above the level of common men are glorified, if not deified, by the people. The whole nation seems to "wonder after these bloody beasts." Grasping ambition, tyrannic usurpation, atrocious aggression, cruel and haughty rule spread and pervade the land. The curse is upon us. The plague is broad. No part of the country can claim entire exemption from its evils. They may be seen as well in the State of New York as in South Carolina; on the Penobscot as on the Sabine.

The people appear to be completely in the hands of office seekers, demagogues, and political gamblers. Within the bewildering meshes of their political nets, they are worried, confused, and confounded, so that a general outcry is heard—"Vigorous prosecution of the war!"—"Mexico must be humbled!"—"Conquer a peace!"—"Indemnity!"—"War forced upon us!"—"National honor!"—"The whole of Mexico!"—"Our destiny!"—"This continent!"—"Anglo-Saxon blood!"—"More territory!"—"Free institutions!"—"Our country!"—till it seems indeed "that justice has fled to brutish beasts and men have lost their reason."

The taste of human blood and the smell of powder seem to have anguished the senses, seared the conscience, and subverted the reason of the people to a degree that may well induce the gloomy apprehension that my nation has fully entered on her downward career and yielded herself up to the revolting idea of battle and blood. "Fire and sword" are now the choice of our young republic. The loss of thousands of her own men, and the slaughter of tens of thousands of the sons and daughters of Mexico, have rather given edge than dullness to our appetite for fiery conflict and plunder. The civilization of the age, the voice of the world, the awareness of human life, the tremendous expense, the dangers, hardships, and the deep disgrace which must forever attach to our inhuman course, seem to oppose no availing check to the mad spirit of proud ambition, blood, and carnage let loose in the land. . . .

—*North Star,* January 21, 1848

12

COLORPHOBIA—A LAW OF NATURE?

Prejudice against color was something Douglass experienced in so many places and situations that it would be impossible to list them all. "Truth is of no color" appeared as part of the slogan he placed on the masthead of the first issue of the North Star. *Even among the antislavery whites who were his colleagues and friends, he noted Jim Crow practices they were not conscious of or failed to resist. In many of his speeches and articles he gave as much attention to racial bias as to slavery. Both were unjust and inseparable. From the moment he arrived in the North as a young fugitive slave, he had encountered Jim Crow. He had no illusions about the innocence of white Northerners.*

PREJUDICE AGAINST COLOR! PRAY TELL US WHAT COLOR? BLACK? BROWN? Copper color? Yellow? Tawny? Or olive? Native Americans of all these colors everywhere experience hourly indignities at the hands of persons claiming to be white. Now, is all this for color's sake? If so, which of these colors excites such commotion in those sallow-skinned Americans who call themselves white? Is it black? When did they begin to be so horrified at black? Was it before black stocks came into fashion? Black coats? Black hats? Black walking canes? Black reticules? Black umbrellas? Black-walnut tables? Black ebony picture frames and sculptural decorations? Black eyes, hair, and whiskers? Bright black shoes, and glossy black horses? How this American colorphobia would have lashed itself into a foam at the sight of the celebrated black goddess Diana of Ephesus! How it would have gnashed upon the old statue and hacked away at it out of sheer spite at its color! What exemplary havoc it would have made of the most celebrated statues of antiquity. Forsooth they were black! Their color would have been their doom. These half-white Americans owe the genius of sculpture a great grudge. She has so often crossed their path in the hated color, it would fare hard with her if she were to fall into their clutches.

By the way, it would be well for Marshall and other European sculptors to keep a keen lookout upon all Americans visiting their collections. American colorphobia would be untrue to itself if it did not pitch battle with every black statue and bust that came in its way in going the rounds. A black Apollo, whatever the symmetry of his proportions, the majesty of his attitude, or the divinity of his air, would meet with great good fortune if it escaped mutilation at its hands, or at least defilement from its spittle. If all foreign artists, whose collections are visited by Americans, would fence off a corner of their galleries for a "Negro pew" and straightway colonize in thither every specimen of ancient and modern art that is chiseled or cast in black, it would be wise precaution.

The only tolerable substitute for such colonization would be plenty of whitewash, which would avail little as a peace offering to brother Jonathan unless freshly put on—in that case a thick coat of it might sufficiently placate his outraged sense of propriety to rescue the finest models of art from American lynch law—but it would not be best to presume too far, for colorphobia has no lucid intervals, the fit is on all the time. The antiblack feeling, being "a law of nature," must have vent; and unless it be provided, wherever it goes, with a sort of portable Liberia to scrape the offensive color into, it twitches and jerks in convulsions directly.

But stop—this antiblack passion is, we are told, "a law of nature," and not to be trifled with! "Prejudice against color," "a law of nature!" Forsooth! What a sinner against nature old Homer was! He goes off in ecstasies in his description of the black Ethiopians, praises their beauty, calls them the favorites of the gods, and represents all the ancient divinities as selecting them from all the nations of the world as their intimate companions, the objects of their peculiar complacency. If Homer had only been indoctrinated into this "law of nature," he would have insulted his deities by representing them as making Negroes their chosen associates. What impious trifling with this sacred "law" was perpetrated by the old Greeks, who represented Minerva, their favorite goddess of wisdom, as an African princess. Herodotus pronounces the Ethiopians the most majestic and beautiful of men. The great father of history was fated to live and die in the dark as to this great "law of nature"!

Why do so many Greek and Latin authors adorn with eulogy the beauty and graces of the black Memnon who served at the siege of Troy, styling him, in their eulogiums, the son of Aurora? Ignoramuses! They knew nothing of this great "law of nature." How little reverence for this sublime "law" had Solon, Pythagoras, Plato, and those other master spirits of ancient Greece, who, in their pilgrimage after knowledge, went to Ethiopia and Egypt and sat at the feet of black philosophers, to drink in wisdom. Alas for the multitudes who flocked from all parts of the world to the instructions of that Negro, Euclid, who, three hundred years before Christ, was at the head of the most celebrated mathematical school in the world. However learned in the mathematics, they were plainly numbskulls in the "law of nature"! . . .

—*North Star*, May 5, 1848

13

The Rights of Women

Perhaps the most important meeting of nineteenth-century reformers took place in July 1848, at Seneca Falls, New York. Planned by Elizabeth Cady Stanton, it was the woman's rights convention, intended to break the chains that bound women. The famous Declaration of Sentiments was read, as well as a resolution declaring it to be "the duty of the women of this country to secure to themselves the sacred right of the elective franchise." Many reformers, including the Garrisonian abolitionists, as well as the country at large, did not approve of giving women the right to vote. But after intense discussion, the resolution was adopted by a small majority. Frederick Douglass, one of thirty-two men at the meeting, cast the lone male vote in favor of it.

Immediately after the convention, Douglass wrote this editorial. He would give lifelong support to women's rights. Remember that the slogan of his North Star was "Right is of no sex—Truth is of no color." He often said that his suffragism came naturally out of his abolitionism: enslaved woman and "woman" were inseparably linked.

ONE OF THE MOST INTERESTING EVENTS OF THE PAST WEEK WAS THE HOLDING of what is technically styled a Woman's Rights Convention at Seneca Falls. The speaking, addresses, and resolutions of this extraordinary meeting was almost wholly conducted by women; and although they evidently felt themselves in a novel position, it is but simple justice to say that their whole proceedings were characterized by marked ability and dignity. No one present, we think, however much he might be disposed to differ from the views advanced by the leading speakers on that occasion, will fail to give credit for brilliant talents and excellent dispositions. In this meeting, as in other deliberative assemblies, there were frequent differences of opinion and animated discussion; but in no case was there the slightest absence of good feeling and decorum. Several interesting documents setting forth the rights as well as the grievances of women were read. Among these was a Declaration of Sentiments, to be regarded as the basis of a grand movement for attaining the civil, social, political, and religious rights of women.

We should not do justice to our own convictions, or to the excellent persons connected with this infant movement, if we did not in this connection offer a few remarks on the general subject which the convention met to consider and the objects they seek to attain. In doing so, we are not insensible that the bare mention of this truly important subject in any other than terms of contemptuous ridicule and scornful disfavor is likely to excite against us the fury of bigotry and the folly of prejudice. A discussion of the rights of animals would be regarded with far more complacency by many of what are called the wise and the good of our land than would a discussion of the rights of women. It is, in their estimation, to be guilty of evil thoughts to think that woman is entitled to equal rights with man. Many who have at last made the discovery that the Negroes have some rights as well as other members of the human family have yet to be convinced that women are entitled to any. Eight years ago a number of persons of this description actually abandoned the antislavery cause, lest by giving their influence in that direction they might possibly be giving countenance to the dangerous heresy that woman, in respect to rights, stands on an equal footing with man. In the judgment of such persons, the American slave system, with all its concomitant horrors, is less to be deplored than this wicked idea.

It is perhaps needless to say that we cherish little sympathy for such sentiments or respect for such prejudices. Standing as we do upon the watchtower of human freedom, we cannot be deterred from an expression of our approbation of any movement, however humble, to improve and elevate the character of any members of the human family. While it is impossible for us to go into this subject at length, and dispose of the various objections which are often urged against such a doctrine as that of female equality, we are free to say that in respect to political rights, we hold woman to be justly entitled to all we claim for man. We go farther and express our conviction that all political rights which it is expedient for man to exercise, it is equally so for woman. All that distinguishes man as an intelligent and accountable being is equally true of woman, and if that government only is just which governs by the free consent of the governed, there can be no reason in the world for denying to woman the exercise of the elective franchise, or a hand in making and administering the laws of the land. Our doctrine is that "right is of no sex." We therefore bid the women engaged in this movement our humble Godspeed.

—*North Star*, July 28, 1848

14

WE MUST BECOME INDEPENDENT

What is the meaning of black independence? In the fall of 1848, Douglass answered that question in a speech to the National Convention of Colored Freemen held at Cleveland, Ohio.

. . . IN THE NORTHERN STATES, WE ARE NOT SLAVES TO INDIVIDUALS, NOT personal slaves, yet in many respects we are the slaves of the community. We are, however, far enough removed from the actual condition of the slave to make us largely responsible for their continued enslavement, or their speedy deliverance from chains. For in the proportion which we shall rise in the scale of human improvement, in that proportion do we augment the probabilities of a speedy emancipation of our enslaved fellow countrymen. It is more than a mere figure of speech to say that we are as a people chained together. We are one people—one in general complexion, one in a common degradation,

one in popular estimation. As one rises, all must rise; and as one falls, all must fall. Having now our feet on the rock of freedom, we must drag our brethren from the slimy depths of slavery, ignorance, and ruin. Every one of us should be ashamed to consider himself free while his brother is a slave. The wrongs of our brethren should be our constant theme. There should be no time too precious, no calling too holy, no place too sacred to make room for this cause. We should not only feel it to be the cause of humanity but the cause of Christianity, and fit work for men and angels.

We ask you to devote yourselves to this cause, as one of the first and most successful means of self-improvement. In the careful study of it, you will learn your own rights and comprehend your own responsibilities and scan through the vista of coming time your high and God-appointed destiny. Many of the brightest and best of our number have become such by their devotion to this cause and the society of white abolitionists. The latter have been willing to make themselves of no reputation for our sake, and in return let us show ourselves worthy of their zeal and devotion. Attend antislavery meetings, show that you are interested in the subject—that you hate slavery and love those who are laboring for its overthrow. Act with white abolition societies wherever you can, and where you cannot, get up societies among yourselves, but without exclusiveness.

It will be a long time before we gain all our rights; and although it may seem to conflict with our views of human brotherhood, we shall undoubtedly for many years be compelled to have institutions of a complexional character in order to attain this very idea of human brotherhood. We would, however, advise our brethren to occupy memberships and stations among white persons and in white institutions, just so fast as our rights are secured to us.

Never refuse to act with a white society or institution because it is white, or a black one because it is black, but act with all men without distinction of color. By so acting we shall find many opportunities for removing prejudices and establishing the rights of all men. We say, avail yourselves of white institutions, not because they are white but because they afford a more convenient means of improvement. . . .

—*North Star*, September 29, 1848

15

INTO THE USEFUL TRADES

While presiding over the National Convention of Colored Freemen at Cleveland, Douglass was asked to write its "Address to the Colored People of the United States." In it he stressed, among other things, the need for African-Americans to gain a greater degree of independence by mastering the trades and by entering farming. It was a theme he would voice again and again for many years.

. . . IN THE CONVENTION THAT NOW ADDRESSES YOU, THERE HAS BEEN MUCH said on the subject of labor, and especially those departments of it with which we as a class have been long identified. You will see by the resolution there adopted on that subject, that the Convention regarded those employments, though right in themselves, as being nevertheless degrading to us as a class, and therefore counsel you to abandon them as speedily as possible and to seek what are called the more respectable employments. While the Convention does not inculcate the doctrine that any kind of needful toil is in itself dishonorable, or that colored persons are to be exempt from what are called menial employments, they do mean to say that such employments have been so long and universally filled by colored men as to become a badge of degradation, in that it has established the conviction that colored men are only fit for such employments. We therefore advise you by all means to cease from such employments, as far as practicable, by pressing into others. Try to get your sons into mechanical trades; press them into the blacksmith's shop, the machine shop, the joiner's shop, the wheelwright's shop, the cooper's shop, and the tailor's shop.

Every blow of the sledgehammer, wielded by a sable arm, is a powerful blow in support of our cause. Every colored mechanic is by virtue of circumstances an elevator of his race. Every house built by black men is a strong tower against the allied hosts of prejudice. It is impossible for us to attach too much importance to this aspect of the subject. Trades are important. Wherever a man may be thrown by misfortune, if he has in his hands a useful trade, he is useful to his fellow man, and will be esteemed accordingly; and of all men in the world who need trades we are the most needy.

Understand this, that independence is an essential condition of respectability. To be dependent is to be degraded. Men may indeed pity us, but they cannot respect us. We do not mean that we can become entirely independent of all men; that would be absurd and impossible in the social state. But we mean that we must become equally independent with other members of the community. That other members of the community shall be as dependent upon us, as we upon them—that such is not now the case is too plain to need an argument. The houses we live in are built by white men, the clothes we wear are made by white tailors, the hats on our heads are made by white hatters, and the shoes on our feet are made by white shoemakers, and the food that we eat is raised and cultivated by white men. Now it is impossible that we should ever be respected as a people while we are so universally and completely dependent upon white men for the necessaries of life. We must make white persons as dependent upon us as we are upon them. This cannot be done while we are found only in two or three kinds of employments, and those employments have their foundation chiefly, if not entirely, in the pride and indolence of the white people. Sterner necessities will bring higher respect.

The fact is, we must not merely make the white man dependent upon us to shave him but to feed him; not merely dependent upon us to black his boots but to make them. A man is only in a small degree dependent on us when he only needs his boots blacked, or his carpetbag carried; as a little less pride and a little more industry on his part may enable him to dispense with our services entirely. As wise men it becomes us to look forward to a state of things which appears inevitable. The time will come when those menial employments will afford less means of living than they now do. What shall a large class of our fellow countrymen do when white men find it economical to black their own boots and shave themselves? What will they do when white men learn to wait on themselves? We warn you, brethren, to seek other and more enduring vocations.

Let us entreat you to turn your attention to agriculture. Go to farming. Be tillers of the soil. On this point we could say much, but the time and space will not permit. Our cities are overrun with menial laborers, while the country is eloquently pleading for the hand of industry to till her soil and reap the reward of honest labor. We beg and entreat you to save your money, live economically, dispense with finery and the gaieties which have rendered us

proverbial—and save your money. Not for the senseless purpose of being better off than your neighbor but that you may be able to educate your children and render your share of the common stock of prosperity and happiness around you. It is plain that the equality which we aim to accomplish can only be achieved by us when we can do for others just what others can do for us. We should, therefore, press into all the trades, professions, and callings into which honorable white men press. . . .

—*North Star*, September 29, 1848

16

A BLOODY OUTBREAK

Mob violence in Northern cities was not uncommon. Pennsylvania, which had the largest black population of any state in the North, was notorious for such outbreaks of racial hatred. Often city officials would collaborate with the mob by making it apparent they'd do nothing to uphold the Constitutional right of peaceable assembly. Or even by furnishing the mob with an excuse, as in this case, when the white Hutchinson Singers insisted on performing before a nonsegregated audience.

THE PAPERS GIVE AN ACCOUNT OF ANOTHER FEROCIOUS MOB IN THIS MOBO-cratic city. Its violence was directed against the colored people in the neighborhood of Sixth and St. Thomas streets—a large number of whom are represented as having been wounded, and ten or twelve as having been killed. As usual, the excuse for this bloody outbreak is represented to be the fact that white and colored persons were living in the same families together and associating on equal terms. One of the papers states that this is a mere pretext. But whether it be true or false it conveys an instructive lesson on the bitterness and baseness of the hatred with which colored people are regarded in Philadelphia. When, in any community, a violation of a mere custom or a disregard of a particular taste is esteemed an available excuse for setting aside all law and for resorting to violence and bloodshed, it shows such custom and taste to be profoundly wedded to the affections of the people, and proves them to be most difficult of eradication.

Slavery and prejudice are evidently above law and order in Philadelphia—and we are not surprised that "the society of killers" should adduce this reason for every outbreak of which they may be guilty. When the mayor of Philadelphia informed the Hutchinson Family [a singing group] that "he could not protect them from the violence of a mob if they permitted colored persons to attend their concerts," he gave up the government, the peace, and the property of that disgraced city into the hands of a band of atrocious mobocrats. They took authority from the hands of the mayor, he virtually telling them that they were to have full liberty to endanger the lives and to destroy the property of any and all persons who should be found acting in disregard of public taste and prejudice by associating, in any way, with colored persons—and thus, also, he marked out the people of color for destruction whenever the brutal propensities of base white men should prompt them to the work of murderous outrage.

The authority has gone from the government of Philadelphia, and the struggle will be long and fearful before it will be regained. Since the burning of Pennsylvania Hall, Philadelphia has been from time to time the scene of a series of most foul and cruel mobs waged against the people of color—and it is now justly regarded as one of the most disorderly and insecure cities in the Union. No man is safe—his life, his property, and all that he holds dear are in the hands of a mob, which may come upon him at any moment, at midnight or midday, and deprive him of his all.

Shame upon the guilty city! Shame upon its lawmakers and law administrators!

—*North Star*, October 19, 1849

17

DO PEOPLE OF COLOR ALL THINK ALIKE?

Douglass sometimes opposed the ideas of Henry Highland Garnet, a distinguished black abolitionist who, like Douglass, had escaped from slavery in Maryland. Garnet, at a public meeting in 1843, called for the slaves to rebel, and Douglass, committed at the time to Garrison's doctrine of nonviolent resistance, opposed

Garnet in a debate. In this reply to questioning readers of his paper, Douglass makes clear that African-Americans have as much right to differ with one another as have whites.

WE HAVE RECEIVED SEVERAL LETTERS RECENTLY, DEPRECATING OUR COURSE toward Henry Highland Garnet and expressing profound regret that differences and controversies should occur among men of the same complexion. We admire the amicability more than we do the sagacity of our correspondents. Until they can prove that sameness of complexion produces harmony of opinion, they will fail to show that colored men have not as good right to differ from each other as have white men. These correspondents and advisers must find a more permanent and rational basis for their regrets than that of "color." The mind does not take its complexion from the skin; to be a colored man is not necessarily to be an abolitionist. . . .

—*North Star*, October 19, 1849

18

THE TRUE LIGHT

Wise legislators, said Douglass, believe that government should strive as far as possible to achieve harmony among all classes of its citizens. Needless insult and injury to any part of its people is unpardonable folly. Yet slaveholding America flouted every precept of good government. In this editorial, Douglass details the many ways by which the government persecuted free blacks.

IT WOULD BE IMPOSSIBLE FOR A GOVERNMENT TO DEVISE A POLICY BETTER calculated to make itself the object of hatred than that adopted by our government toward its free colored people. To make us detest the land of our birth—to abhor the government under which we live—and to welcome the approach of an invading enemy as our only salvation would seem to be the animating spirit and purpose of all the legislative enactments of the country with respect to us. With all its boasted wisdom and dignity, it does not hesitate to use every opportunity of persecuting, insulting, and assailing the weakest and most defenseless part of its subjects or citizens. It acts toward us as though the highest crime we could commit is that of patriotism, and all manner of insult, neglect, and contempt are necessary to prevent the commission of this crime on our part. Our thoughts have been turned in this direction by the contemptible meanness of our present secretary of state, in refusing to grant to William W. Brown the usual passport granted to citizens about to travel in foreign countries. Mr. Brown remarks (in a recent letter to Mr. Garrison) that one of his fellow passengers to Europe was accompanied by a colored servant, and that this servant had with him a regular passport, signed by the secretary of state, Mr. Buchanan.

This fact presents the American government in its true light. It has no objection whatever to extend its protection to colored servants, but it is resolved on no occasion to grant protection to colored gentlemen. A colored man who travels for the benefit of a white man will have thrown over him a shield and panoply of the United States; but, if he travels for his own profit or pleasure, he forfeits all the immunities of an American citizen. The government, in this particular, fairly reflects the lights and shades of the whole American mind: as appendages to white men we are universally esteemed; as independent and responsible men we are universally despised.

In keeping with this spirit, and in pursuance of this policy, the colored man is not permitted to carry a United States mailbag across the street, nor hand it from a stage driver to a postmaster. In the navy, no matter how great may be his talents, skill, and acquirements—no matter how daring, heroic, and patriotic he may be—he is forbidden, by the government, to rise above the office of a cook or a steward under the flag of the United States.

The colored man, if a slave, may travel in company with his master into any state or territory in the Union; but if he be a free man, he may not even visit the capital of the nation (which he helps to support by his taxes) without the liability of being cast into prison, kept there for months together, and then taken out and sold like a beast of burden under the auctioneer's hammer for his jail fees. Besides the gross frauds and ruinous wrongs heaped with scandalous profusion on the heads of the colored people by the government, the white population at large (saints and sinners) is constantly exerting its skill and ingenuity in devising schemes which serve to embitter our lot and to destroy our happiness.

From places of instruction and amusement, open to all other nations under the sun, we are excluded; from the cabins of steamboats and the tables of hotels (which are free to English, Irish, Dutch, Scotch, and also to the most rude Hoosier of the West) we are excluded; from the ecclesiastical convention and the political caucus, we are generally excluded; from the bar and jury box of our country, we are excluded; from respectable trades and employments, and from nearly all the avenues to wealth and power, we are excluded; from the Lyceum Hall and the common school, the sources of light and education, we are as a people excluded.

Meanwhile, societies are organized under the guise of philanthropy and religion, whose chief business it is to propagate the most malignant slanders against us and to keep up in the public mind a violent animosity between us and our white fellow citizens. Upon this the government smiles with approbation and exerts its utmost powers to execute the behests of this unnatural and cruel prejudice. What is this but the most discreditable disregard of sound political wisdom, to say nothing of the dictates of justice and magnanimity? Can the colored man be expected to entertain for such a government any feelings but those of intense hatred? Or can he be expected to do other than to seize the first moment which shall promise him success to gratify his vengeance? To apprehend that he would not do so would evince the most deplorable ignorance of the elements of human nature.

We warn the American people, and the American government, to be wise in their day and generation. The time may come that those whom they now despise and hate may be needed. Those compelled foes may by and by be wanted as friends. America cannot always sit as a queen, in peace and repose. Prouder and stronger governments than hers have been shattered by the bolts of the wrath of a just God. We beseech her to have a care how she goads the sable oppressed in the land. We warn her, in the name of retribution, to look to her ways, for in an evil hour those hands that have been engaged in beautifying and adorning the fair fields of our country may yet become the instruments of spreading desolation, devastation, and death throughout our borders.

—*North Star,* November 9, 1849

19

HERE WE ARE, AND HERE WE STAY

Colonization—a scheme launched by prominent white slaveholders at the beginning of the 1800s—was opposed by Douglass from his earliest speeches on. He scorned the idea of deporting his people. Their native land was here, and here they meant to stay. Conventions of African-Americans, year by year, adopted resolutions opposing plans for repatriation in Africa. Under strong attack by free blacks and by white abolitionists, colonization eventually died. Fewer than fifteen thousand blacks left American shores. In 1849, Douglass wrote this editorial on the issue.

IT IS IMPOSSIBLE TO SETTLE, BY THE LIGHT OF THE PRESENT AND BY THE experience of the past, anything, definitely and absolutely, as to the future condition of the colored people of this country. But so far as present indications determine, it is clear that this land must continue to be the home of the colored man so long as it remains the abode of civilization and religion. For more than two hundred years we have been identified with its soil, its products, and its institutions; under the sternest and bitterest circumstances of slavery and oppression, under the lash of slavery at the South, under the sting of prejudice and malice at the North, and under hardships the most unfavorable to existence and population, we have lived, and continue to live and increase.

The persecuted red man of the forest, the original owner of the soil, has step by step retreated from the Atlantic lakes and rivers; escaping, as it were, before the footsteps of the white man and gradually disappearing from the face of the country. He looks upon the steamboats, the railroads, and canals cutting and crossing his former hunting grounds and upon the ploughshare throwing up the bones of his venerable ancestors and beholds his glory departing—and his heart sickens at the desolation. He spurns the civilization—he hates the race which has despoiled him—and unable to measure arms with his superior foe, he dies.

Not so with the black man. More unlike the European in form, feature, and color—called to endure greater hardships, injuries, and insults than those to which the Indians have been subjected, he yet lives and prospers under every disadvantage. Long have his enemies sought to expatriate him and to teach his children that this is not their home, but in spite of all their cunning schemes and subtle contrivances, his footprints yet mark the soil of his birth, and he gives every indication that America will, forever, remain the home of his posterity. We deem it a settled point that the destiny of the colored man is bound up with that of the white people of this country; be the destiny of the latter what it may.

It is idle—worse than idle—ever to think of our expatriation, or removal. The history of the colonization society must extinguish all such speculations. We are rapidly filling up the number of four millions; and all the gold of California combined would be insufficient to defray the expenses attending our colonization. We are, as laborers, too essential to the interests of our white fellow countrymen to make a very grand effort to drive us from this country among probable events. While labor is needed, the laborer cannot fail to be valued; and although passion and prejudice may sometimes vociferate against us and demand our expulsion, such efforts will only be spasmodic and can never prevail against the sober second thought of self-interest.

We are here, and here we are likely to be. To imagine that we shall ever be eradicated is absurd and ridiculous. We can be remodified, changed, and assimilated, but never extinguished. We repeat, therefore, that we are here; and that this is our country; and the question for the philosophers and states-men of the land ought to be, What principles should dictate the policy of the action toward us? We shall neither die out nor be driven out, but shall go with this people, either as a testimony against them, or as an evidence in their favor throughout their generations. We are clearly on their hands and must remain there forever. All this we say for the benefit of those who hate the Negro more than they love their country. . . .

—*North Star,* November 16, 1849

20

PERISH ALL SHOWS OF KINDNESS

To the frequent refrain that slavemasters—at least some of them—were kind to their slaves, Douglass had this to say. He was replying to a letter from the owner of 122 slaves in Mississippi, who read the North Star *and objected to its "indiscriminate abuse of slaveholders."*

. . . YOU DOUBTLESS THINK THAT SOMETHING IS DUE TO KIND MASTERS AND perhaps rank yourself among the number. To all such we say, kind or cruel, you are bound to quit your grasp on your slaves. You have no right but the right of a robber to your victims. Your fancied kindness, to what does it amount when set against the loss of liberty, the loss of progress, the loss of the means of education, and the overwhelming degradation to which the slave is subjected—the mere packhorse of another—a man transformed into a beast of burden—a name which might be enrolled among the blest on the Lamb's Book of Life, sacrilegiously degraded to a place in the pages of your ledger with horses, sheep, and swine? Perish all shows of kindness when they are thought to conceal or to palliate the damning character of slavery.

—*North Star*, April 12, 1850

21

A HELL-BORN HATRED

Prejudice against color, said Douglass, "is the greatest of all obstacles in the way of the antislavery cause." The heartless apathy prevailing in the community on the subject of slavery obliged him to report on prejudice and relentlessly examine its every aspect. Here he offers an acute analysis of what prejudice is and how it operates.

. . . PROPERLY SPEAKING, PREJUDICE AGAINST COLOR DOES NOT EXIST IN THIS country. The feeling (or whatever it is), which we call prejudice, is no less than a murderous, hell-born hatred of every virtue which may adorn the character of a black man. It is not the black man's color which makes him the object of brutal treatment. When he is drunken, idle, ignorant, and vicious, "Black Bill" is a source of amusement: he is called a good-natured fellow; he is the first to [give] service in holding his horse, or blacking his boots. The white gentleman tells the landlord to give "Bill" "something to drink," and actually drinks with "Bill" himself!—While poor black "Bill" will minister

to the pride, vanity, and laziness of white American gentlemen—while he consents to play the buffoon for their sport, he will share their regard.

But let him cease to be what we have described him to be—let him shake off the filthy rags that cover him—let him abandon drunkenness for sobriety, indolence for industry, ignorance for intelligence, and give up his menial occupation for respectable employment—let him quit the hotel and go to the church and assume there the rights and privileges of one for whom the Son of God died, and he will be pursued with the fiercest hatred. His name will be cast out as evil; and his life will be embittered with all the venom which hate and malice can generate. Thousands of colored men can bear witness to the truth of this representation. While we are servants, we are never offensive to the whites or marks of popular displeasure. We have been often dragged or driven from the tables of hotels where colored men were officiating acceptably as waiters; and from steamboat cabins where twenty or thirty colored men in light jackets and white aprons were frisking about as servants among the whites in every direction. On the very day we were brutally assaulted in New York for riding down Broadway in company with ladies, we saw several white ladies riding with black servants. These servants were well-dressed, proud-looking men, evidently living on the fat of the land—yet they were servants. They rode not for their own but for the pleasure and convenience of white persons. They were not in those carriages as friends or equals—they were there as appendages; they constituted a part of the magnificent equipages. They were there as the fine black horses which they drove were there—to minister to the pride and splendor of their employers. As they passed down Broadway, they were observed with admiration by the multitude; and even the poor wretches who assaulted us might have said in their hearts as they looked upon such splendor, "We would do so too if we could."

We repeat, then, that color is not the cause of our persecution; that is, it is not our color which makes our proximity to white men disagreeable. The evil lies deeper than prejudice against color. It is, as we have said, an intense hatred of the colored man when he is distinguished for any ennobling qualities of head or heart. If the feeling which persecutes us were prejudice against color, the colored servant would be as obnoxious as the colored gentleman, for the color is the same in both cases; and being the same in both cases, it would produce the same result in both cases.

We are then a persecuted people not because we are colored but simply because that color has for a series of years been coupled in the public mind with the degradation of slavery and servitude. In these conditions, we are thought to be in our place; and to aspire to anything above them is to contradict the established views of the community—to get out of our sphere and commit the provoking sin of impudence. Just here is our sin: we have been a slave; we have passed through all the grades of servitude and have, under God, secured our freedom; and if we have become the special object of attack, it is because we speak and act among our fellow men without the slightest regard to their or our own complexion; and further, because we claim and exercise the right to associate with just such persons as are willing to associate with us, and who are agreeable to our tastes and suited to our moral and intellectual tendencies, without reference to the color of their skin, and without giving ourselves the slightest trouble to inquire whether the world is pleased or displeased by our conduct. We believe in human equality; that character, not color, should be the criterion by which to choose associates; and we pity the pride of the poor pale dust and ashes which would erect any other standard of social fellowship.

This doctrine of human equality is the bitterest yet taught by the abolitionists. It is swallowed with more difficulty than all the other points of the antislavery creed put together. "What, make a Negro equal to a white man? No, we will never consent to that! No, that won't do!" But stop a moment; don't be in a passion; keep cool. What is a white man that you do so revolt at the idea of making a Negro equal with him? Who made an angel of a man? "A man." Very well, he is a man, and nothing but a man—possessing the same weaknesses, liable to the same diseases, and under the same necessities to which a black man is subject. Wherein does the white man differ from the black? Why, one is white and the other is black. Well, what of that? Does the sun shine more brilliantly upon the one than it does upon the other? Is nature more lavish with her gifts toward the one than toward the other? Do earth, sea, and air yield their united treasures to the one more readily than to the other? In a word, "have we not all one Father?" Why then do you revolt at that equality which God and nature instituted?

The very apprehension which the American people betray on this point is proof of the fitness of treating all men equally. The fact that they fear an acknowledgment of our equality shows that they see a fitness in such an acknowledgment. Why are they not apprehensive lest the horse should be placed on an equality with man? Simply because the horse is not a man; and no amount of reasoning can convince the world, against its common sense, that the horse is anything else than a horse. So here all can repose without fear. But not so with the Negro. He stands erect. Upon his brow he bears the seal of manhood, from the hand of the living God. Adopt any mode of reasoning you please with respect to him, he is a man, possessing an immortal soul, illuminated by intellect, capable of heavenly aspirations, and in all things pertaining to manhood, he is at once self-evidently a man, and therefore entitled to all the rights and privileges which belong to human nature.

—*North Star*, June 13, 1850

22

A Letter to American Slaves

In 1850, Douglass wrote a public "Letter to American Slaves from Those Who Have Fled from American Slavery." Addressing them as "Afflicted and Beloved Brothers," he spoke in behalf of all runaway slaves like himself. The letter gave an honest picture of the difficult life of African-Americans in the North yet still encouraged flight and promised whatever help was possible. He then made these suggestions for those who managed to reach the North.

. . . There are three points in your conduct, when you shall have become inhabitants of the North, on which we cannot refrain from admonishing you.

First: If you will join a sectarian church, let it not be one which approves of the Negro pew and which refuses to treat slaveholding as a high crime against God and man. It were better that you sacrifice your lives than that by going into the Negro pew, you invade your self-respect, debase your souls, play the traitor to your race, and crucify afresh Him who died for the one brotherhood of man.

Second: Join no political party which refuses to commit itself fully, openly, and heartfully—in its newspapers, meetings, and nominations—to the doctrine that slavery is the grossest of all absurdities as well as the guiltiest of all abominations and that there can no more be a law for the enslavement of man made in the image of God than for the enslavement of God himself. Vote for no man for civil office who makes your complexion a bar to political, ecclesiastic, or social equality. Better die than insult yourself and insult our social equality. Better die than insult yourself and insult every person of African blood—and insult your Maker—by contributing to elevate to civil office he who refuses to eat with you, to sit by your side in the House of Worship, or to let his children sit in the school by the side of your children.

Third: Send not your children to the school which the malignant and murderous prejudice of white people has gotten up exclusively for colored people. Valuable as learning is, it is too costly if it is acquired at the expense of such self-degradation.

The self-sacrificing and heroic and martyr-spirit, which would impel the colored men of the North to turn their backs on proslavery churches and proslavery politics and proslavery schools, would exert a far mightier influence against slavery than could all their learning, however great, if purchased by concessions of their manhood and surrenders of their rights and coupled, as it then would be, by characteristic meanness and servility. . . .

—*North Star*, September 5, 1850

23

A GIGANTIC EVIL

Early in December 1850, Douglass began a series of lectures on American slavery, delivered in Rochester's Corinthian Hall. He noted that many prominent people had done their best "to complicate, mystify, entangle, and obscure the simple truth" about slavery. These "wise and great ones" had so twisted the popular mind and corrupted the public heart that it was time to offer a "calm, candid, and faithful discussion" of the subject. His first lecture demonstrated the dominating influence of slavery on the affairs of the nation.

. . . A VERY SLIGHT ACQUAINTANCE WITH THE HISTORY OF AMERICAN SLAVERY is sufficient to show that it is an evil of which it will be difficult to rid this country. It is not the creature of a moment, which today is and tomorrow is not; it is not a pygmy, which a slight blow may demolish; it is no youthful upstart, whose impertinent pratings may be silenced by a dignified contempt. No: it is an evil of gigantic proportions, and of long standing. . . .

. . . Allow me to speak of the nature of slavery itself; and here I can speak, in part, from experience—I can speak with the authority of positive knowledge. . . .

First of all, I will state, as well as I can, the legal and social relation of master and slave. A master is one (to speak in the vocabulary of the Southern states) who claims and exercises a right of property in the person of a fellow man. This he does with the force of the law and the sanction of Southern religion. The law gives the master absolute power over the slave. He may work him, flog him, hire him out, sell him, and, in certain contingencies, kill him, with perfect impunity. The slave is a human being, divested of all rights, reduced to the level of a brute, a mere "chattel" in the eye of the law, placed beyond the circle of human brotherhood, cut off from his kind; his name, which the "recording angel" may have enrolled in heaven among the blest, is impiously inserted in a master's ledger with horses, sheep, and swine. In law, the slave has no wife, no children, no country, and no home. He can own nothing, possess nothing, acquire nothing but what must belong to another. To eat the fruit of his own toil, to clothe his person with the work of his own hands, is considered stealing. He toils, that another may reap the fruit; he is industrious, that another may live in idleness; he eats unbolted meal, that another may eat the bread of fine flour; he labors in chains at home, under a burning sun and a biting lash, that another may ride in ease and splendor abroad; he lives in ignorance, that another may be educated; he is abused, that another may be exalted; he rests his toil-worn limbs on the cold, damp ground, that another may repose on the softest pillow; he is clad in coarse and tattered raiment, that another may be arrayed in purple and fine linen; he is sheltered only by the wretched hovel, that a master may dwell in a magnificent mansion; and to this condition he is bound down as by an arm of iron.

From this monstrous relation there springs an unceasing stream of most revolting cruelties. The very accompaniments of the slave system stamp it as the offspring of hell itself. To ensure good behavior, the slaveholder relies on the whip; to induce proper humility, he relies on the whip; to rebuke what he is pleased to term insolence, he relies on the whip; to supply the place of wages as an incentive to toil, he relies on the whip; to bind down the spirit of the slave, to imbrute and to destroy his manhood, he relies on the whip, the chain, the gag, the thumbscrew, the pillory, the bowie knife, the pistol, and the bloodhound. These are the necessary and unvarying accompaniments of the system. . . .

Nor is slavery more adverse to the conscience than it is to the mind. This is shown by the fact that in every state of the American Union where slavery exists, except the state of Kentucky, there are laws absolutely prohibitory of education among the slaves. The crime of teaching a slave to read is punishable with severe fines and imprisonment and, in some instances, with death itself.

Nor are the laws respecting this matter a dead letter. Cases may occur in which they are disregarded, and a few instances may be found where slaves may have learned to read; but such are isolated cases, and only prove the rule. The great mass of slaveholders look upon education among the slaves as utterly subversive of the slave system. I well remember when my mistress first announced to my master that she had discovered that I could read. His face colored at once, with surprise and chagrin. He said that I was ruined, and my value as a slave destroyed; that a slave should know nothing but to obey his master; that to give a Negro an inch would lead him to take an ell; that having learned how to read, I would soon want to know how to write; and that, by and by, I would be running away. I think my audience will bear witness to the correctness of this philosophy, and to the literal fulfillment of this prophecy.

It is perfectly well understood at the South that to educate a slave is to make him discontented with slavery and to invest him with a power which shall open to him the treasures of freedom; and since the object of the slaveholder is to maintain complete authority over his slave, his constant vigilance is exercised to prevent everything which militates against or endangers the stability of his authority. Education being among the menacing influences and, perhaps, the most dangerous, is, therefore, the most cautiously guarded against.

It is true that we do not often hear of the enforcement of the law, punishing as crime the teaching of slaves to read, but this is not because of a want of disposition to enforce it. The true reason, or explanation of the matter is this: there is the greatest unanimity of opinion among the white population of the South in favor of the policy of keeping the slave in ignorance. There is, perhaps, another reason why the law against education is so seldom violated. The slave is too poor to be able to offer a temptation sufficiently strong to induce a white man to violate it; and it is not to be supposed that in a community where the moral and religious sentiment is in favor of slavery, many martyrs will be found sacrificing their liberty and lives by violating those prohibitory enactments.

As a general rule, then, darkness reigns over the abodes of the enslaved, and "how great is that darkness!"

We are sometimes told of the contentment of the slaves and are entertained with vivid pictures of their happiness. We are told that they often dance and sing; that their masters frequently give them wherewith to make merry; in fine, that they have little of which to complain. I admit that the slave does sometimes sing, dance, and appear to be merry. But what does this prove? It only proves, to my mind, that though slavery is armed with a thousand stings, it is not able entirely to kill the elastic spirit of the bondsman. That spirit will rise and walk abroad, despite whips and chains, and extract from the cup of nature occasional drops of joy and gladness. No thanks to the slaveholder, nor to slavery, that the vivacious captive may sometimes dance in his chains, his very mirth in such circumstances stands before God as an accusing angel against his enslaver. . . .

—*North Star*, December 5, 1850

24

LET THE HEAVENS WEEP!

The 1850s were a time of great turmoil. It was the decade in which two great questions—whether slavery could be ended and whether the Union could survive— became central in the American mind. For African-Americans it marked a new stage in the long struggle to achieve freedom and equality. Each passing year witnessed setbacks—passage of the Fugitive Slave Act and the Kansas-Nebraska Act, and the Dred Scott decision handed down by the Supreme Court.

Black leaders, of course, could not foresee the coming of the Civil War, which would destroy slavery. For them the 1850s were a dismal time, almost a time of despair. The reliance by many on moral persuasion to win white America to the cause of emancipation seemed a failure. It had produced few practical results. Yet Douglass clung to a stoic faith in the possibility of peaceful change. He never failed in his speeches and writings to hold out hope to his people.

The first great shock of the decade came when Congress adopted the Compromise of 1850. It was an attempt to find a middle ground that would appease both North and South and unite the nation. The territories carved from the lands taken from Mexico would decide the slavery question for themselves. The foreign slave trade was ended, but not slavery in the District of Columbia. And a new and harsher fugitive slave law was proposed that would force the North to return runaways to their masters. On September 18, 1850, it became law.

Despair and panic swept over the African-Americans in the North. Probably fifty thousand fugitives had found shelter above the Mason-Dixon line. Many had married free blacks. Now none were safe. Thousands fled overnight to Canada. For free blacks, a reign of terror had begun.

In April 1851, a Georgia slavemaster showed up in Boston to claim seventeen-year-old Thomas Sims as his slave. Immediately, black and white abolitionists made plans to effect a forcible rescue of Sims. They failed to save him. This is how Douglass saw the events.

LET THE HEAVENS WEEP AND LET HELL BE MERRY! SLAVERY HAS TRIUMPHED! Daniel Webster has at last obtained from Boston, the cradle of liberty, a living sacrifice to appease the slave God of the American Union. A man guilty of no crime—and charged with none—has been seized at the point of the bayonet and doomed to a lot more terrible than death. From the heights of freedom, he has been hurled into the depths of slavery, to gratify three of the most infernal propensities of man's malicious heart—pride, avarice, and revenge. Yes! We say revenge—bloodthirsty, murderous revenge. Had not this been the actuating motive, the victim might have been ransomed. Money could have sacrificed avarice, success might have soothed wounded pride;

nothing can appease a slaveholder's revenge but the torn back and warm blood of his helpless victim.

Thomas [Sims] is to be made an example of, to deter slaves from escaping the hateful house of bondage. He is to be tortured for the amusement of his tormentors and to strike terror to the hearts of his trembling companions in bondage. It is Boston—civilized, refined, Christian, and humane Boston—that has furnished this sacrifice! Great God! Wilt thou not visit for these things? Wilt thou not be avenged on such a nation as this?

Amid the deep distress and anguish which this sad occurrence has brought us, there are points of consolation connected with it which, while they do not help the man now on the highway to slavery, serve to mitigate the disheartening effect of his surrender. He was carried off to slavery, yet not with ease. He was overcome, yet not without a struggle, both on his own part and on the part of his friends. As soon as he found himself in the hands of a legalized kidnapper, he drew out his knife and stabbed the villain, although not fatally. Overcome by superior force, he was imprisoned in the courthouse to prevent a rescue on the part of his friends. The temple of justice was literally surrounded by chains and bayonets.

The horrid men-hunters only escaped a deserved death by the precaution of never allowing themselves to walk forth in broad daylight unprotected by an armed police, and the government (strong and mighty as it is) did not even venture to confront the burning indignation of the traveling public of New England, by taking the innocent man in fetters, by the usual traveling conveyances through the land; but under cover of night (like a band of pirates on the coast of Africa), they hurried their victim off to the lonely sea, surrounded by hired ruffians armed to the tooth, were towed away from the sight of humanity by a steamer provided for the purpose. . . .

—*Frederick Douglass' Paper*, April 17, 1851

25

THE RIGHTS OF WOMAN AND MAN ARE IDENTICAL

In the following two extracts from Douglass's writings we can see additional expression of his progressive views on women's rights. The first comments on a

woman's rights convention held in Worcester, Massachusetts, in 1851. The second, written in 1853, supports women's right to the ballot.

. . . IN OUR EYES, THE RIGHTS OF WOMAN AND THE RIGHTS OF MAN ARE identical—we ask no rights, we advocate no rights for ourselves, which we would not ask and advocate for woman. Whatever may be said as to a division of duties and avocations, the rights of man and the rights of woman are one and inseparable and stand upon the same indestructible basis. If, for the well being and happiness of man, it is necessary that he should hold property, have a voice in making the laws which he is expected to obey, be stimulated by his participation in government to cultivate his mental faculties, with a view to an honorable fulfillment of his social obligations, precisely the same may be said of woman.

We advocate woman's rights, not because she is an angel but because she is a woman, having the same wants and being exposed to the same evils as man.

Whatever is necessary to protect him is necessary to protect her. Holding these views, and being profoundly desirous that they should universally prevail, we rejoice at every indication of progress in their dissemination.

—*Frederick Douglass' Paper,* October 30, 1851

. . . NO MAN COULD LISTEN TO MISS STONE'S ADDRESS ON SUNDAY EVENING without feeling that there was much reason in her speech, and in no part of it more than in that she portrayed the perfect dearth of motive and object afforded by society to young ladies. It was shown that on leaving school, about the most which is expected of a young lady is that she will go home and "do little pretty things to wear"—nothing more.

This is all wrong; a woman should have every honorable motive to exertion which is enjoyed by man, to the full extent of her capacities and endowments. The case is too plain for argument. Nature has given woman the same powers, and subjected her to the same earth, she breathes the same air, subsists on the same food—physical, moral, mental, and spiritual. She has, therefore, an equal right with man, in all efforts to obtain and maintain a perfect existence.

. . . Woman, however, like the colored man, will never be taken by her brother and lifted to a position. What she desires, she must fight for. With her as with us, "Who would be free themselves must strike the blow." The price demanded for the good sought is labor, self-sacrifice, the loss of popularity, loss of the good opinions of men. It is only when the object shall, in estimation, transcend all these that the effort will be commensurated with the conditions of success.

Does woman think she can build a house, and that that is the best appropriation of her time and the best application of her strength and talents? We say, let her go at it, and let shame fall upon the man who would hinder by word or deed the laudable undertaking. But we repeat woman must practically, as well as theoretically, assert her rights. She must do, as well as be. A Doctor Harriot K. Hunt, a Reverend Antoinette L. Brown, or a Mrs. Paulina Davis, all actively exercising the rights for which they contend, are proof against a world's sophistry and a world's ridicule. It is only in the heat of battle that balls lose their terror. So far as employments are concerned, the coast is comparatively clear, and woman can manage the matter for herself. But not so in the matter of voting. Men must do the work here. They must, like true men and true democrats, batter down the thick walls erected against woman at the ballot box and let taxation and representation go together.

—*Frederick Douglass' Paper*, June 10, 1853

26

WHEN WRITTEN IN BLOOD

For some time vital changes had been fermenting in Douglass's mind. Together with other black and white abolitionists, he came to believe that appeals to moral force were plainly not effective. They turned to politics as the field on which the war against slavery had to be fought. This ran counter to Garrison's rejection of political action. He saw the Constitution and the political system it sustained as the hopeless tools of slavery.

Beginning in the 1840s, Douglass slowly drifted away from the Garrisonians.

He was influenced in part by his friend Gerrit Smith, who had long adopted an antislavery interpretation of the Constitution. Smith held that the document empowered Congress to end slavery in the Southern states by direct legislation. By mid-1851 Douglass was completely converted to a radical antislavery view of the Constitution as the legal foundation for the earlier promise of the Declaration of Independence.

A supporter of the North Star *during its thirteen years, Smith had helped Douglass to replace it with a new publication, called* Frederick Douglass' Paper. *It threw its support to the struggling Liberty Party. Douglass promoted its local, state, and national activities and carried articles by its leading theorists. That fall he was elected to its national committee.*

The new paper did moderately well, losing some Garrisonian subscribers but gaining new ones. It was Smith's monthly subsidy that enabled it to provide a decent living for the staff and for the Douglass family.

Late in 1851, Douglass reviewed a new collection of Garrison's speeches and writings, and while praising his early mentor, drew distinctions between his own views and Garrison's.

. . . IN REGARD TO THE DOCTRINE OF NONPHYSICAL RESISTANCE TO EVIL, SO eloquently maintained by Mr. Garrison, we reject it, with deference, to be sure, but with a full conviction of its unsoundness. The only "peace" principle which we are able to comprehend is justice. We contend that he who does most to establish this principle does most to establish "Peace on earth and goodwill toward men," and further, without at all dispensing with or losing faith in moral force, we hold that physical resistance to evil has often been and is now a solemn duty in the sight of God and man. In short, it is evident that when oppressors and tyrants silence all appeals in behalf of justice and mercy, blot out all right rules for the guidance of man toward man, and consult only their own selfish pride and pleasure, he is a benefactor of all mankind and the servant of the God of Peace, who traces the straight line of immutable justice with the blood of such oppressors and tyrants, as a warning to all who would trample in the dust the precious lights of human nature. The time for "nonresistance" has not yet come. There are lessons needful to mankind, which will be learned only when written in blood; and however it may be deplored, it is which can secure "peace" to the sons of man. Where there are oppression and slavery, there can be no "peace," and the removal of these, it seems to us, will never be effected until tyrants are taught that it is perilous to stand upon the quivering heartstrings of outraged humanity. . . .

—*Frederick Douglass' Paper,* January 29, 1852

27

WHAT IS YOUR FOURTH OF JULY TO ME?

One of Douglass's most celebrated speeches was his "Fourth of July Address" in 1852, in Rochester, New York. Speaking to a crowded antislavery audience of his white neighbors, he urged them to cling to the Fourth of July as "the first great fact of your nation's history," when the claim to life, liberty, and the pursuit of happiness for all Americans was so thrillingly declared in the words of Thomas Jefferson. But "the Fourth of July is yours, not mine," *he went on. "You* may *rejoice; I* must mourn."

After examining at great length America's hypocritical democracy, he challenged his listeners with this passionate outcry.

FELLOW CITIZENS: PARDON ME, AND ALLOW ME TO ASK, WHY AM I CALLED upon to speak here today? What have I or those I represent to do with your national independence? Are the great principles of political freedom and of natural justice, embodied in that Declaration of Independence, extended to us? And am I, therefore, called upon to bring our humble offering to the national altar and to confess the benefits and express devout gratitude for the blessings resulting from your independence to us?

What to the American slave is your Fourth of July? I answer, a day that reveals to him, more than all other days of the year, the gross injustice and cruelty to which he is the constant victim. To him your celebration is a sham; your boasted liberty an unholy license; your national greatness, swelling vanity; your sounds of rejoicing are empty and heartless; your denunciation of tyrants, brass-fronted impudence; your shouts of liberty and equality, hollow mockery; your prayers and hymns, your sermons and thanksgivings, with all your religious parade and solemnity, are to him mere bombast, fraud, deception, impiety, and hypocrisy—a thin veil to cover up crimes which would disgrace a nation of savages. There is not a nation of the earth guilty of practices more shocking and bloody than are the people of these United States at this very hour.

Go where you may, search where you will, roam through all the monarchies and despotisms of the Old World, travel through South America, search out every abuse, and when you have found the last, lay your facts by the side of the everyday practices of this nation, and you will say with me that, for revolting barbarity and shameless hypocrisy, America reigns without a rival. . . .

—"Oration delivered in Corinthian Hall,
Rochester, New York," July 5, 1852

28

WORK—OR DIE

Watching free blacks crowded out of their traditional jobs by newly arrived white immigrants, Douglass urged the establishment of apprenticeships and training schools to prepare his people for the trades and skilled industrial crafts. It was a theme he would continue to stress for decades to come.

THE OLD AVOCATIONS BY WHICH COLORED MEN OBTAINED A LIVELIHOOD ARE rapidly, unceasingly, and inevitably passing into other hands; every hour sees the black man elbowed out of employment by some newly arrived emigrant, whose hunger and whose color are thought to give him a better title to the place; and so we believe it will continue to be until the last prop is leveled beneath us.

As a black man, we say if we cannot stand up, let us fall down. We desire to be a man among men while we do live; and when we cannot, we wish to die. It is evident, painfully evident to every reflecting mind, that the means of living, for colored men, are becoming more and more precarious and limited. Employments and callings formerly monopolized by us are so no longer.

White men are becoming house servants, cooks, and stewards, on vessels, at hotels. They are becoming porters, stevedores, wood-sawyers, hod-carriers, brickmakers, white-washers, and barbers, so that the blacks can scarcely find the means of subsistence; a few years ago, and a white barber would have been a curiosity—now their poles stand on every street. Formerly blacks were almost the exclusive coachmen in wealthy families: this is so no longer; white men are now employed, and for aught we see, they fill their servile station with an obsequiousness as profound as that of the blacks. The readiness and ease with which they adapt themselves to these conditions ought not to be lost sight of by the colored people. The meaning is very important, and we should learn it. We are taught our insecurity by it. Without the means of living, life is a curse and leaves us at the mercy of the oppressor to become his debased slaves.

Now, colored men, what do you mean to do, for you must do something? We tell you to go to work; and to work you must go or die. Men are not valued in this country, or in any country, for what they are; they are valued for what they can do. It is in vain that we talk about being men if we do not the work of men. We must become valuable to society in other departments of industry than those servile ones from which we are rapidly being excluded. We must show that we can do as well as be; and to this end we must learn trades. When we can build as well as live in houses; when we can make as well as wear shoes; when we can produce as well as consume wheat, corn, and rye—then we shall become valuable to society.

Society is a hard-hearted affair. With it the helpless may expect no higher dignity than that of paupers. The individual must lay society under obligation to him, or society will honor him only as a stranger and sojourner. How shall this be done? In this manner: use every means, strain every nerve, to master some important mechanical art. At present, the facilities for doing this are few—institutions of learning are more readily opened to you than the work-shop; but the Lord helps them who will help themselves, and we have no doubt that new facilities will be presented as we press forward.

If the alternative were presented to us of learning a trade or of getting an education, we would learn the trade, for the reason that with the trade we could get the education, while with the education we could not get the trade. What we, as a people, need most is the means for our own elevation. An

educated colored man, in the United States, unless he has within him the heart of a hero and is willing to engage in a lifelong battle for his rights as a man, finds few inducements to remain in this country. He is isolated in the land of his birth—debarred by his color congenial association with whites, he is equally cast out by the ignorance of the blacks. The remedy for this must comprehend the elevation of the masses; and this can only be done by putting the mechanic arts within the reach of colored men.

We have now stated pretty strongly the case of our colored countrymen; perhaps, some will say, too strong, but we know whereof we affirm.

In view of this state of things, we appeal to the abolitionists. What boss antislavery mechanic will take a black boy into his wheelwright's shop, his blacksmith's shop, his joiner's shop, his cabinet shop? Here is something practical; where are the whites and where are the blacks that will respond to it? Where are the antislavery milliners and seamstresses that will take colored girls and teach them trades by which they can obtain an honorable living? The fact that we have made good cooks, good waiters, good barbers, and white-washers induces the belief that we may excel in higher branches of industry. One thing is certain: we must find new methods of obtaining a livelihood, for the old ones are failing us very fast.

We, therefore, call upon the intelligent and thinking ones amongst us to urge upon the colored people within their reach, in all seriousness, the duty and the necessity of giving their children useful and lucrative trades by which they may commence the battle of life with weapons commensurate with the exigencies of the conflict.

—*Frederick Douglass' Paper,* March 4, 1853

29

''No Colored Person Admitted''

The vocal talent of Elizabeth Taylor Greenfield, born in Mississippi, was early recognized by a Quaker woman who took her to Philadelphia for training. On the concert stage she became known as "The Black Swan," achieving considerable fame. She was compared favorably with the greatest sopranos of her time, such as

Jenny Lind. She toured the free states and Canada and then, in 1853, left for Europe, where she continued her career as singer and teacher. But her eminence did not let her escape the criticism of Douglass for giving in to Jim Crow.

HOW MEAN, BITTER, AND MALIGNANT IS PREJUDICE AGAINST COLOR! IT IS THE most brainless, brutal, and inconsistent thing of which we know anything. It can dine heartily on dishes prepared by colored hands. It can drink heartily from the glass filled by colored hands. It can snooze soundly under a razor guided by colored hands. Finally, it can go to Metropolitan Hall and listen with delight to the enchanting strains of a black woman—if in all those relations there be conditions acknowledging the inferiority of black people to white. This brainless and contemptible creature, neither man nor beast, caused the following particular notice to be placed on the placard announcing the concert of "The Black Swan" in Metropolitan Hall, New York:

> Particular Notice: No colored person can be admitted, as there is no part of the house appropriated for them.

We marvel that Miss Greenfield can allow herself to be treated with such palpable disrespect, for the insult is to her not less than to her race.

She must have felt deep humiliation and depression while attempting to sing in the presence of an audience and under arrangements which had thus degraded and dishonored the people to which she belongs. Oh! That she could be a woman as well as a songstress, brave and dauntless, resolved to fall or flourish with her outraged race, to scorn the mean propositions of the oppressor, and refuse sternly to acquiesce in her own degradation. She is quite mistaken if she supposes that her success as an artist depends upon her entire abandonment of self-respect. There are generous hearts enough in this country who, if she but led the way, would extend to her the meed of praise and patronage commensurate with her merits. We warn her also that this yielding on her part to the cowardly and contemptible exactions of the Negro haters of this country may meet her in a distant land in a manner which she little imagines.

—*Frederick Douglass' Paper*, April 8, 1853

30

THE GOALS OF OUR ENEMIES

In a speech to the annual meeting of the American and Foreign Anti-slavery Society in May 1853 in New York, Douglass underscored the proslavery agreement of both major political parties. Each had put up candidates in the recent 1852 presidential election, but it made little difference to African-Americans which side won. And ominously, state legislatures in the North were echoing what was being done in Washington on the great issue.

. . . It is evident that there is in this country a purely slavery party; a party which exists for no other earthly purpose but to promote the interests of slavery. The presence of this party is felt everywhere in the republic. It is known by no particular name and has assumed no definite shape, but its branches reach far and wide in the church and in the state. This shapeless and nameless party is not intangible in other and more important respects. That party has determined upon a fixed, definite, and comprehensive policy toward the whole colored population of the United States. What that policy is, it becomes us as abolitionists, and especially does it become the colored people themselves, to consider and understand fully. We ought to know who our enemies are, where they are, and what are their objects and measures.

Well, here is my version of it; not original with me but mine because I hold it to be true. I understand this policy to comprehend five cardinal objects. They are these:

First: The complete suppression of all antislavery discussion.
Second: The expatriation of the entire free people of color from the United States.
Third: The unending perpetuation of slavery in this republic.
Fourth: The nationalization of slavery to the extent of making slavery respected in every state of the Union.
Fifth: The extension of slavery over Mexico and the entire South American states.

These objects are forcibly presented to us in the stern logic of passing events—in the facts which are and have been passing around us during the last three years. The country has been and is now dividing on these grand issues. In their magnitude these issues cast all others into the shade, depriving them of all life and vitality. Old party lines are broken. Like is finding its like on either side of these great issues, and the great battle is at hand. For the present, the best representative of the slavery party in politics is the Democratic Party. Its great head for the present is President Pierce, whose boast it is that his whole life has been consistent with the interests of slavery; that he is above reproach on that score. In his inaugural address he reassures the South on this point. The head of the slave power being in power, it is natural that the proslavery elements should cluster around the administration, and this is rapidly being done. . . .

The keystone to the arch of this grand union of the slavery party of the United States is the Compromise of 1850. In that compromise we have all the objects of our slaveholding policy specified. It is favorable to this view of the designs of the slave power that both the Whig and the Democratic parties bent lower, sunk deeper, and strained harder in their conventions, preparatory to the late presidential election, to meet the demands of the slavery party than at any previous time in their history. Never did parties come before the Northern people with propositions of such undisguised contempt for the moral sentiment and the religious ideas of that people. They virtually asked them to unite in a war upon free speech, upon conscience, and to drive the Almighty Presence from the councils of the nation. Resting their platforms upon the Fugitive Slave Bill, they boldly asked the people for political power to execute the horrible and hell-black provisions of that bill.

The history of that election reveals with great clearness the extent to which slavery has shot its leprous distillment through the lifeblood of the nation. The party most thoroughly opposed to the cause of justice and humanity triumphed, while the party suspected of a leaning toward liberty was over-whelmingly defeated—some say, annihilated. But here is a still more important fact illustrating the designs of the slave power. It is a fact full of meaning that no sooner did this Democratic leading party come into power than a system of legislation was presented to the legislatures of the Northern states, designed to put the states in harmony with the Fugitive Slave Law and the malignant bearing of the national government toward the colored inhabitants of the country. This whole movement on the part of the states bears the evidence of having one origin, emanating from one head, and urged forward by one power. It was simultaneous, uniform, and general, and looked to one end. It was intended to put thorns under feet already bleeding, to crush a people already bowed down, to enslave a people already but half free. In a word, it was intended to discourage, dishearten, and drive the free colored people out of the country. . . .

—Annual Report of the American and
Foreign Anti-slavery Society for 1853

31

WHAT WE ASK

A convention of free blacks held in Rochester, New York, in the summer of 1853 examined the general condition of African-Americans. A committee was appointed to prepare an address to the American people at large, stating the claims of blacks as fellow citizens under a government set up to protect, not to destroy, the rights of all the people. Douglass drew up the address, from which these passages are taken.

WE ASK THAT IN OUR NATIVE LAND, WE SHALL NOT BE TREATED AS STRANGERS, and worse than strangers.

We ask that, being friends of America, we should not be treated as enemies of America.

We ask that, speaking the same language and being of the same religion, worshiping the same God, owing our redemption to the same Savior, and learning our duties from the same Bible, we shall not be treated as barbarians.

We ask that, having the same physical, moral, mental, and spiritual wants common to other members of the human family, we shall also have the same means which are granted and secured to others to supply those wants.

We ask that the doors of the schoolhouse, the workshop, the church, the college shall be thrown open as freely to our children as to the children of other members of the community.

We ask that the American government shall be so administered as that beneath the broad shield of the Constitution, the colored American seaman shall be secure in his life, liberty, and property in every state in the Union.

We ask that as justice knows no rich, no poor, no black, no white, but, like the government of God, renders alike to every man reward or punishment according as his works shall be, the white and black man may stand upon an equal footing before the laws of the land.

We ask that (since the right of trial by jury is a safeguard to liberty, against the encroachments of power, only as it is a trial by impartial men, drawn indiscriminately from the country) colored men shall not, in every instance, be tried by white persons; and that colored men shall not be either by custom or enactment excluded from the jury box.

We ask that (inasmuch as we are, in common with other American citizens, supporters of the State, subject to its laws, interested in its welfare, liable to be called upon to defend it in time of war, contributors to its wealth in time of peace) the complete and unrestricted right of suffrage, which is essential to the dignity even of the white man, be extended to the free colored man also.

Whereas the colored people of the United States have too long been retarded and impeded in the development and improvement of their natural faculties and powers, even to become dangerous rivals to white men in the honorable pursuits of life, liberty, and happiness; and whereas, the proud Anglo-Saxon can need no arbitrary protection from open and equal competition with any variety of the human family; and whereas, laws have been enacted limiting the aspirations of colored men as against white men—we respectfully submit that such laws are flagrantly unjust to the man of color and plainly discreditable to white men; and for these and other reasons, such laws ought to be repealed.

We especially urge that all laws and usages which preclude the enrollment of colored men in the militia, and prohibit their bearing arms in the navy, disallow their rising, agreeable to their merits and attainments, are unconstitutional—the Constitution knowing no color—are anti-Democratic, since democracy respects men as equals, are unmagnanimous, since such laws are made by the many against the few and by the strong against the weak.

We ask that all those cruel and oppressive laws, whether enacted at the South or the North, which aim at the expatriation of the free people of color, shall be stamped with national reprobation, denounced as contrary to the humanity of the American people, and as an outrage upon the Christianity and civilization of the nineteenth century.

We ask that the right of preemption, enjoyed by all white settlers upon the public lands, shall also be enjoyed by colored settlers; and that the word *white* be struck from the preemption act. We ask that no appropriations whatever, state or national, shall be granted to the colonization scheme; and we would have our right to leave or to remain in the United States placed above legislative interference.

We ask that the Fugitive Slave Law of 1850—that legislative monster of modern times, by whose atrocious provisions the writ of "habeas corpus," the "right of trial by jury," have been virtually abolished—shall be repealed.

We ask that the Law of 1793 be so construed as to apply only to apprentices and others really owing service or labor; and not to slaves, who can owe nothing. Finally, we ask that slavery in the United States shall be immediately, unconditionally, and forever abolished.

To accomplish these just and reasonable ends, we solemnly pledge ourselves to God, to each other, to our country, and to the world, to use all and every means consistent with the just rights of our fellow men and with the precepts of Christianity.

We shall speak, write and publish, organize and combine to accomplish them.

We shall appeal to the Church and to the government to gain them.

We shall vote and expend our money to gain them.

We shall send eloquent men of our own condition to plead our cause before the people.

We shall invite the cooperation of good men in this country and throughout the world—and above all, we shall look to God, the Father and Creator of all men, for wisdom to direct us and strength to support us in the holy cause to which we this day solemnly pledge ourselves.

—"The Claims of Our Coming Cause: Address of the Colored Convention,
    Rochester, New York, July 1853, to the People of the United States"

32

TIME TO WAKE UP!

Speaking to a lyceum audience in Manchester, New Hampshire, Douglass made the case for interpreting the Constitution as an antislavery document. He criticized those abolitionists (the Garrisonians) who had "too easily given up the Constitution to slavery." He insisted on the principle of the illegality of slavery and the government's power to abolish it everywhere.

Then he went on to justify the use of force by any fugitive slave who seeks to break free of his pursuer and appealed to his Northern listeners to resist the attempts of the slave power to control them.

Douglass had made his home in Rochester, New York, a reliable stop on the underground railroad. Runaway slaves heading for Canada spent their last night in the slaveholding United States hidden in his house or barn. At dawn, they would be sent on their way to free land across the border.

. . . I FEEL I WALK NOW NOT ON A FREE SOIL. THE STAR-SPANGLED BANNER affords no protection. The Fugitive Slave Bill covers the whole country. The slave may be started from the far west and chased to the far east; there is no valley so deep, no mountain so high, no plain so boundless, no glen so secluded, no cave so secure, no spot so sacred, as to give him shelter from the bloodhound and hunter. He may pass into the New England states, to Concord and Bunker Hill, and ascend that shaft, and ask in the name of the first blood that was shed at its base for protection, and even there, the hungry, biting bloodhound and the master with his accursed chains can go and snatch the bondman away. They can do it right under the eave droppings of old Fanueil Hall, and under the stately spires of your magnificent churches.

We are told the Fugitive Slave Law is constitutional; that there is a clause in the Constitution that authorizes the recapture of slaves. But the clause is not there. When it says "no person shall be deprived of life, liberty, or property without due process of law" it looks right. Men have tried to see a recognition of this law there, but it is not. I used to think it was there, but like the Irishman's flea, "when I put my finger on it, it wasn't thar." But there is an article in the Constitution that declares "no person, held to service or labor in one state under the laws thereof, shall in consequence of any law be released from such service or labor, and shall be delivered up," which article was intended to secure to every man what is due to him. Mr. Webster, in his seventh of March speech, said this clause of the Constitution was introduced in consequence of a widespread system of apprenticeship and on account of a large class of redemptioners that existed at that time. There is nothing there to leave the impression that it was intended for the recapture of slaves. And it is a strange fact that not until the lapse of twenty-five years was a slave returned from the North to the South. This fugitive law is a modern invention; we have constitutions outside of the Constitution. I believe in denying everything to slavery and claiming everything for liberty.

Some men have supposed every law proslavery until it has been proved otherwise; they proceed on the presumption that the Constitution is in favor of slavery. The great mistake of the antislavery men of modern times is that they have too easily given up the Constitution to slavery. If our fathers introduced a clause into it for the purpose to return the bondman, then they transcended their authority, they leaped out of the orbit of their rights. Had your fathers any right to make slaves? Look over your rights, and have you one which gives you liberty to make a slave of your brother man? If you have not, your fathers had not, and they had no right to command others to make them. Suppose in some fit of generosity I should write each of you a title deed, giving you three hundred acres of clear blue sky, all full of stars. What then? Why, the stars would stay up there and shine as bright as ever; the sky would not fall down. You could not appropriate it to yourself. So if I should give you a title deed to own somebody else as property, would your right to that person hold good? You may pile statutes to the heavens, affirming the right of one class of men to hold another in servitude, yet they will be null and void.

Now we have the Fugitive Slave Law, how shall we get rid of it? I do not think it will ever be repealed; it is too low and bad for that. It is not only to be trampled upon and disregarded but scorned and scouted at by every man and woman. It was enacted for the basest of purposes; it was to humble you; to make you feel that the South could command you and make you run on the track of the bondman and hunt him down.

A law of this kind is to be met with derision, and if the poor slave, escaping

from his pursuer, shall find himself unable to get beyond the reach of the tyrant, and he should turn around and strike him down to the earth, there is something in the heart of universal manhood that will say, "You served the villain right."

This law goes directly against religious liberty. We hear much about religious liberty in Tuscany, Rome, and Russia, but you can point to no law in Russia, Turkey, Austria, or any of the Papal states that can equal this law in its warfare against religious liberty if this liberty means the liberty to practice Christianity. The law tells you good ministers and elders, "We shall expect you to forget the law of God at the ballot box and enforce the law of the Devil." To be sure it does not strike down any of the ordinances of religion, but it strikes down man. There is no other system of religion so benevolent and merciful as Christianity! It reaches down its long, benevolent arm through every grade of suffering and seizes the last link in the chain and says, "Stand up, thou art a man and brother." But this law makes Christianity a crime; it has made the law of God an outlaw. It tells ministers they shall no longer learn their duty to their fellow men from the Bible but from the statute book. There comes the slave from Alabama. He comes in the dark night—he dare not trust himself if by moonlight—he travels toward the North Star:

> Star of the North, I ask to thee.
> While on I press—for well I know
> Thy light and truth shall make me free
> Thy light, which no poor slave deceiveth,
> Thy light, which all my soul believeth.

On he comes, he reaches us, he comes to the door of a Christian and says, "Give me bread and shelter or I die"; but the law of the country says, if you do that, you shall have a home in a cold, damp cell and shall see the light of day through granite windows for six months, besides paying a fine of $1,000.

I wish Americans did not love office so well. It is strange how fascinating it is, however mean it may be. How many men at the North have made shipwreck of their principles, honor, and everything else while listening to the promise of office! It makes me think of a dog I once saw. A fellow held up a biscuit before him and said "Speak," and the dog spoke. "Stand up," and he stood up. "Roll over," and he did so; and the fellow, very complacently, put the biscuit in his pocket and said, "Now go and lay down." This is the way Southerners have treated Northern statesmen. They have told them to "speak," and they have stood up and spoken for slavery. They then said "Roll over," and they have rolled over and cast off their old principles of freedom. Then they say, "Go and lay down forever—you are of no further service." It is time Northern men should wake up. There is no need of allowing the slave power to control you any longer. It is degradation intensified for you to suffer yourselves to be the vassals of women whippers and the dupes of Northern aspirants for office and power.

—*Frederick Douglass' Paper*, February 10, 1854

33

A COVENANT WITH DEATH

Early in 1854, there was furious public debate over the Kansas-Nebraska Bill, introduced by Senator Stephen A. Douglas. It called for organization of the two new territories under the doctrine of "popular sovereignty." If adopted by Congress, it would end the Missouri Compromise of 1820, which called for no slavery in territories north of Missouri's southern border.

Frederick Douglass wrote this editorial against the bill, demolishing both it and the Missouri Compromise as giveaways to the slaveholders. Despite the efforts of the abolitionists, the bill became law on May 30, 1854.

. . . THIS COMPROMISE OF 1820 CAN ONLY BE INSISTED UPON NOW, BY THE North, on the low ground of "honor among thieves," or at best, as the least of two evils. It was a compromise at the first—has been ever since—and is now, and will be so long as it is permitted to exist, "not fit to be made." It was a demoralizing bargain and has done more to debauch the moral sentiment of the nation than any other legislative measure we know of. In the face of the universality of the principles of justice, humanity, and religion, it would localize and legalize a crime against humanity only second in turpitude to murder itself. In no degree is that compromise less offensive to us because it halts at positive avowal and accomplishes what we allege of it by inference only. The inference in this instance is practically as mischievous as would have been a substantive declaration authorizing the establishment of slavery south of 36° 30'. To say that slavery should not be established north of this line was equal to saying that it might be established south of it. So the South understood the bargain at the time, and so the North understood it at the time. There is no getting away from it. Whatever may be said of other compacts, this, at least, was a "covenant with death" and one which cannot be innocently perpetuated by this generation. Those who made it had no right to make it; and we who live after them have no right to keep it. The fact that now a proposition comes from the slavery side for its repeal shows the danger of ever making compacts with wrong. It is another illustration of thawing a deadly viper instead of killing it.

We regard this Missouri Compromise as scarcely fit to be made an incidental issue with the slave power. It may be owing to our ignorance of, and our want of experience in, matters of this sort—but to our unsophisticated apprehension, the friends of freedom have but little real concern for the Missouri Compromise, or any other compromise with the slave power of the country. Our cause is not helped, but hindered, by pleading such compromises. That cause must fight its battles on broader and sounder principles than can be found in the narrow and rotten Compromise of 1820. Liberty must stick no stakes and draw no lines short of the outer circle of the republic. Liberty and justice, as laid down in the preamble of the U.S. Constitution, must be maintained in the outermost parts of the republic.

The real issue to be made with the slave power, and the one which should never be lost sight of, is this: Slavery, like rape, robbery, piracy, or murder, has no right to exist in any part of the world—that neither north or south of 36° 30' shall it have a moment's repose if we can help it. On this vantage ground, the friends of freedom are impregnable. On any other, they are easily put to flight. Slavery can beat us in talking of lines and compromises. Most plainly we are lame here, even though our side shall be better than theirs. They have more talkers and more backers than we; and what they lack in the goodness of their cause they make up in these. . . .

To us, the attempt now being made in Congress to nullify the Missouri

Compromise is hateful because it is designed to extend and perpetuate slavery. Herein is the essential wrong, and against the man-imbruting, labor-degrading, land-blasting curse of curses and crime of crimes should all the batteries of freedom be directed. The struggle is one for ascendancy. Slavery aims at absolute sway and to banish liberty from the republic. It would drive out the schoolmaster and install the slavedriver, burn the schoolhouse and erect the whipping post, prohibit the Holy Bible and establish the bloody slave code, dishonor free labor with its hope of reward and establish slave labor with its dread of the lash. This is the crusade of cruelty and blood guiltiness which the friends of freedom are now called upon to resist, and not the perfidy or bad faith involved in repealing the rotten Compromise of 1820.

The mere repeal of that compromise apart from such objects as are now contemplated, standing alone, is a thing to which the friends of freedom might, so far as we are able to see, properly assent. It is more irrepealable than any other human enactment. If slavery does not repeal it, freedom ought and will in the end. The fact that its repeal is now sought in a fraudulent manner, and from the blackest of motives, and for the basest of purposes, should not make us lose sight of the real nature of the compromise itself and hold it as a thing desirable. While it exists, liberty fights slavery over a chain. A hand-to-hand struggle is more desirable. Let the two systems of free labor and slave labor meet and decide the great question between them fairly, without congressional or executive interference, and freedom would have nothing to lose in such a contest.

If nonintervention were really to be hoped for from the passing of this Nebraska bill, slavery would gain nothing by it. Let but this general government cease to interfere in behalf of slavery. Let the compromises into which it has entered be repealed, and slavery stand out, distinct from national politics, nakedly upon its own merits, and it would disappear like the dew before the brightness of the morning sun. Slavery is now protected under the shadow of the national government. The slaveholder has heretofore found his greatest security in pleading the past in support of his claims. Old compromises, old understandings, old intentions, and so forth have been his covert and refuge. Now let him destroy his covert and refuge, if he will, and the consequences be on his own head. . . .

—*Frederick Douglass' Paper*, February 24, 1854

34

IT'S TIME FOR A GREAT NEW PARTY OF FREEDOM

When the Kansas-Nebraska Act finally became law in May 1854, Douglass and others called for the formation of a new political party that would stand firmly on a platform to abolish slavery. In July, the Republican Party was formed out of a realignment of political forces in the North and West. It opposed the extension of slavery into the territories. In October, speaking in his state of Illinois, Lincoln also condemned the Kansas-Nebraska Act and denounced slavery. While it did not call for complete abolition of slavery and equal rights for blacks, Douglass placed his hopes on the new party's future.

AGAINST THE INDIGNANT VOICE OF THE NORTHERN PEOPLE—AGAINST THE commonest honesty—against the most solemn warnings from statesmen and patriots—against the most explicit and public pledges of both the great parties—against the declared purpose of President Pierce on assuming the reins of government—against every obligation of honor and the faith of mankind—against the stern resistance of a brave minority of our representatives—against the plainest dictates of the Christian religion and the voice of its ministers, the hell-black scheme for extending slavery over Nebraska, where thirty-four years ago it was solemnly protected from slavery forever, has triumphed. The audacious villainy of the slave power and the contemptible pusillanimity of the North have begotten this monster and sent him forth to blast and devour whatsoever remains of liberty, humanity, and justice in the land. The North is again whipped—driven to the wall. . . .

But what is to be done? Why, let this be done: let the whole North awake, arise; let the people assemble in every free state of the Union; and let a great party of freedom be organized, on whose broad banner let it be inscribed, "All compromises with slavery ended—the abolition of slavery essential to the preservation of liberty." Let the old parties go to destruction, whither they have nearly sunk the nation. Let their names be blotted out and their memory rot; and henceforth let there be only a free party, and a slave party.

The time for action has come. While a grand political party is forming, let companies of emigrants from the free states be collected together—funds provided—and with every solemnity which the name and power of God can inspire. Let them be sent out to possess the goodly land, to which, by a law of Heaven and a law of man, they are justly entitled.

—*Frederick Douglass' Paper*, May 26, 1854

35

TO KILL A KIDNAPPER

Perhaps the most famous of the many attempts at rescue of a fugitive slave occurred in Boston in May 1854. Anthony Burns had escaped from his Virginia master in February and was hiding in Boston, sheltered by the black community. He was arrested on May 24 and placed under guard in the courthouse. Word of his capture spread quickly, and the antislavery forces plotted his rescue. During their attack on the courthouse, James Batchelder, a truckman who had volunteered to serve as U.S. Marshal, was killed. President Pierce ordered out troops to force the return of Burns to slavery. The military and the police carried Burns down to the dock through a crowd of fifty thousand people crying and hissing "Shame!" Burns was flung into the hold of a ship bound for Virginia.

While recognizing that the shedding of human blood was regarded by decent people with horror, Douglass argued that resistance to slavehunters was both reasonable and right.

. . . THE OCCURRENCE NATURALLY BRINGS UP THE QUESTION OF THE REASONableness and the rightfulness of killing a man who is in the act of forcibly reducing a brother man, who is guilty of no crime, to the horrible condition of a slave. The question bids fair to be one of important and solemn interest, since it is evident that the practice of slave-hunting and slave-catching, with all their attendant enormities, will either be pursued indefinitely or abandoned immediately, according to the decision arrived at by the community. . . .

We take it to be a sound principle that when government fails to protect

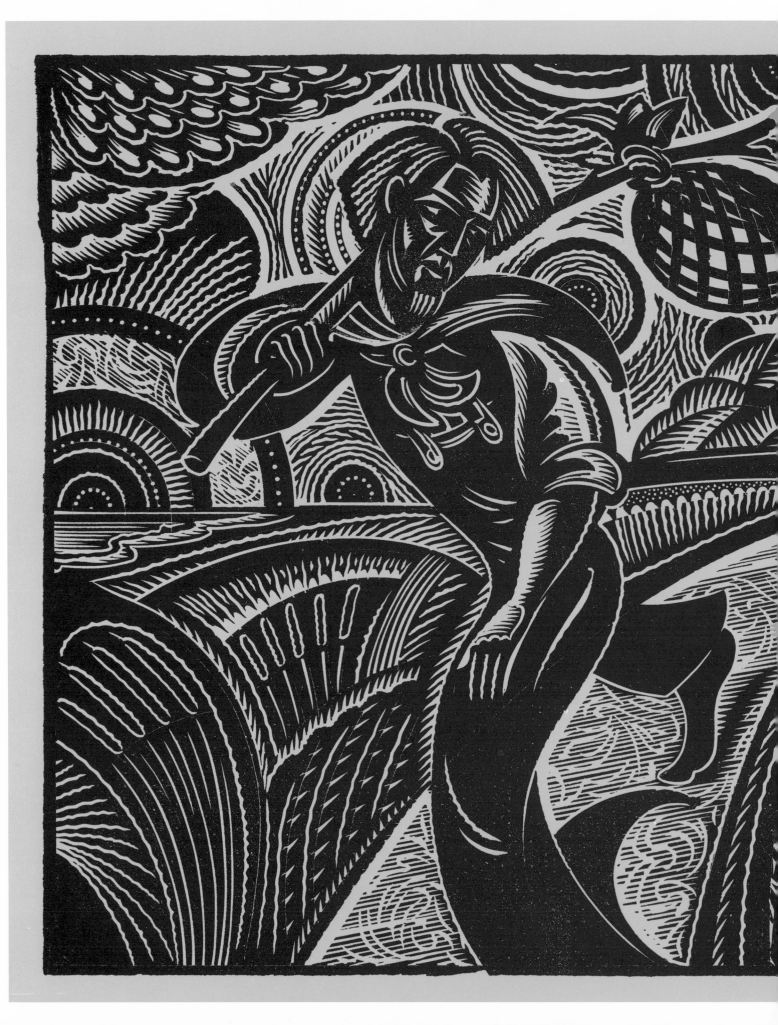

the just rights of any individual man, either he or his friends may be held in the sight of God and man innocent in exercising any right for his preservation which society may exercise for its preservation. Such an individual is flung, by his untoward circumstances, upon his original right of self-defense. We hold, therefore, that when James Batchelder, the truckman of Boston, abandoned his useful employment as a common laborer and took upon himself the revolting business of a kidnapper and undertook to play the bloodhound on the track of his crimeless brother Burns, he labeled himself the common enemy of mankind, and his slaughter was as innocent in the sight of God as would be the slaughter of a ravenous wolf in the act of throttling an infant. We hold that he had forfeited his right to live and that his death was necessary as a warning to others liable to pursue a like course.

It may be said that though the right to kill in defense of one's liberty be admitted, it is still unwise for the fugitive slave or his friends to avail themselves of this right; and that submission, in the circumstances, is far wiser than resistance. To this it is a sufficient answer to show that submission is valuable only so long as it has some chance of being recognized as a virtue. While it has this chance, it is well enough to practice it, as it may then have some moral effect in restraining crime and shaming aggression, but no longer. That submission on the part of the slave has ceased to be a virtue is very evident. While fugitives quietly cross their hands to be tied, adjust their ankles to be chained, and march off unresistingly to the hell of slavery, there will ever be fiends enough to hunt them and carry them back. Nor is this all nor the worst. Such submission, instead of being set to the credit of the poor sable ones, only creates contempt for them in the public mind and becomes an argument in the mouths of the community that Negroes are, by nature, only fit for slavery; that slavery is their normal condition. Their patient and unresisting disposition, their unwillingness to peril their own lives by shooting down their pursuers, is already quoted against them as marking them as an inferior race. This reproach must be wiped out, and nothing short of resistance on the part of colored men can wipe it out. Every slave-hunter who meets a bloody death in his infernal business is an argument in favor of the manhood of our race. Resistance is, therefore, wise as well as just. . . .

—*Frederick Douglass' Paper*, June 2, 1854

36

ONE MAN, WITH RIGHT ON HIS SIDE

Although Douglass's whole-souled devotion to the cause of emancipation was un-questionable, he could still view its course over the years with a critical eye. In a lecture before the Rochester Ladies' Anti-Slavery Society in January 1855, he analyzed the various antislavery sects and parties. Among them he took up the Garrisonian division, and especially attacked its doctrine of "No Union with Slaveholders."

. . . ITS PECULIAR AND DISTINCTIVE FEATURE IS ITS DOCTRINE OF "NO UNION with slaveholders." This doctrine has, of late, become its bond of union and the condition of good fellowship among its members. Of this society, I have to say, its logical result is but negatively antislavery. Its doctrine of "no union with slaveholders" carried out, dissolves the Union and leaves the slaves and their masters to fight their own battles, in their own way. This I hold to be an abandonment of the great idea with which that society started. It started to free the slave. It ends by leaving the slave to free himself. It started with the purpose to imbue the heart of the nation with sentiments favorable to the abolition of slavery, and ends by seeking to free the North from all responsibility of slavery, other than if slavery were in Great Britain or under some other nationality.

This, I say, is the practical abandonment of the idea with which that society started. It has given up the faith that the slave can be free short of the overthrow of the government; and then, as I understand that society, it leaves the slaves, as it must needs leave them, just where it leaves the slaves of Cuba, or those of Brazil. The nation, as such, is given up as beyond the power of salvation by the foolishness of preaching; and hence, the aim is now to save the North; so that the American Anti-Slavery Society, which was inaugurated to convert the nation, after ten years' struggle parts with its faith and aims now to save the North. . . .

I dissent entirely from this reasoning. It assumes to be true what is plainly absurd, and that is that a population of slaves—without arms, without means of concert, and without leisure—is more than a match for double its number, educated, accustomed to rule, and in every way prepared for warfare, offensive or defensive. This society, therefore, consents to leave the slave's freedom to a most uncertain and improbable, if not an impossible, contingency.

But, "no union with slaveholders."

As a mere expression of abhorrence of slavery, the sentiment is a good one; but it expresses no intelligible principle of action and throws no light on the pathway of duty. Defined as its authors define it, it leads to false doctrines and mischievous results. It condemns Gerrit Smith for sitting in Congress and our Savior for eating with publicans and sinners. Dr. Spring uttered a shocking sentiment when he said if one prayer of his would emancipate every slave, he would not offer that prayer. No less shocking is the sentiment of the leader of the disunion forces, when he says that if one vote of his would emancipate every slave in this country, he would not cast that vote. Here, on a bare theory, and for a theory which, if consistently adhered to, would drive a man out of the world—a theory which can never be made intelligible to common sense—the freedom of the whole slave population would be sacrificed. . . .

—The Anti-Slavery Movement: A Lecture of Frederick Douglass, before Rochester Ladies' Anti-Slavery Society, Rochester, New York, 1855

37

SHALL SLAVES SUBMIT FOREVER?

As the 1850s saw setback after setback for the abolitionists—the Fugitive Slave Act, the Kansas-Nebraska Act, and soon the Dred Scott decision—Douglass became convinced that there was little chance slavery would be ended peacefully. In a period of despair, he predicted what the end would be, and the coming of the Civil War—four years later—would prove him right.

WHILE WE FEEL BOUND TO USE ALL OUR POWERS OF PERSUASION AND ARGUMENT; to welcome every instrumentality that promises to peacefully destroy that perpetual contemner of God's laws and disturber of a nation's peace— Slavery; we yet feel that its peaceful annihilation is almost hopeless, and hence stand by the doctrines enunciated in those resolutions, and contend that the

slave's right to revolt is perfect, and only wants the occurrence of favorable circumstances to become a duty. . . . We cannot but shudder as we call to mind the horrors that have ever marked servile insurrections—we would avert them if we could; but shall the millions forever submit to robbery, to murder, to ignorance, and every unnamed evil which an irresponsible tyranny can devise because the overthrow of that tyranny would be productive of horrors? We say not. The recoil, when it comes, will be in exact proportion to the wrongs inflicted; terrible as it will be, we accept and hope for it. The slaveholder has been tried and sentenced, his execution only waits the finish to the training of his executioners. He is training his own executioners.
—William Chambers, *American Slavery and Color*, New York, 1857

38

THIS INFAMOUS DECISION

On March 6, 1857, Chief Justice Roger B. Taney handed down the Supreme Court's decision on the case of Dred Scott. Scott was a household slave of an army surgeon taken by his master from Missouri, a slave state, into Illinois, a free state, and then into Wisconsin Territory, where slavery was banned by the Missouri Compromise. Scott sued for his liberty on the ground that he had become free because of his temporary residence on free soil.

What Taney's decision meant was spelled out by Douglass in this speech he gave to the American Abolition Society in Rochester, in May 1857. Note how he struggles to maintain hope in his people.

The decision made the slaveholders jubilant. But in the North and West, great mass meetings were held in furious protest against the decision. White voters and politicians—like Abraham Lincoln—were driven in ever larger numbers toward the antislavery movement.

. . . This infamous decision of the slaveholding wing of the Supreme Court maintains that slaves are, within the contemplation of the Constitution of the United States, property; that slaves are property in the same sense that horses, sheep, and swine are property; that the old doctrine that slavery is a creature of local law is false; that the right of the slaveholder to his slave does not depend upon the local law but is secured wherever the Constitution of the United States extends; that Congress has no right to prohibit slavery anywhere; that slavery may go in safety anywhere under the star-spangled banner; that colored persons of African descent have no rights that white men are bound to respect; that colored men of African descent are not and cannot be citizens of the United States.

You will readily ask me how I am affected by this devilish decision—this judicial incarnation of wolfishness? My answer is, and no thanks to the slave-holding wing of the Supreme Court, my hopes were never brighter than now.

I have no fear that the national conscience will be put to sleep by such an open, glaring, and scandalous tissue of lies as that decision is and has been, over and over, shown to be.

The Supreme Court of the United States is not the only power in this world. It is very great, but the Supreme Court of the Almighty is greater. Judge Taney can do many things, but he cannot perform impossibilities. He cannot bail out the ocean, annihilate the firm old earth, or pluck the silvery star of liberty from our northern sky. He may decide, and decide again; but he cannot reverse the decision of the Most High. He cannot change the essential nature of things—making evil good, and good evil.

Happily for the whole human family, their rights have been defined, declared, and decided in a court higher than the Supreme Court. "There is a law," says Brougham, "above all the enactments of human codes, and by that law, unchangeable and eternal, man cannot hold property in man."

Your fathers have said that man's right to liberty is self-evident. There is no need of argument to make it clear. The voices of nature, of conscience, of reason, and of revelation, proclaim it as the right of all rights, the foundation of all trust and of all responsibility. Man was born with it. It was his before he comprehended it. The deed conveying it to him is written in the center of his soul and is recorded in Heaven. The sun in the sky is not more palpable to the sight than man's right to liberty is to the moral vision. To decide against this right in the person of Dred Scott, or the humblest and most whip-scarred bondman in the land, is to decide against God. It is an open rebellion against God's government. It is an attempt to undo what God has done, to blot out the broad distinction instituted by the Allwise between

men and things, and to change the image and superscription of the ever-living God into a speechless piece of merchandise.

Such a decision cannot stand. God will be true though every man be a liar. We can appeal from this hell-black judgment of the Supreme Court to the court of common sense and common humanity. We can appeal from man to God. If there is no justice on earth, there is yet justice in Heaven. You may close your Supreme Court against the black man's cry for justice, but you cannot, thank God, close against him the ear of a sympathizing world nor shut up the Court of Heaven. All that is merciful and just, on earth and in Heaven, will execrate and despise this edict of Taney.

If it were at all likely that the people of these free states would tamely submit to this demoniacal judgment, I might feel gloomy and sad over it, and possibly it might be necessary for my people to look for a home in some other country. But as the case stands, we have nothing to fear.

In one point of view, we, the abolitionists and colored people, should meet this decision, unlooked for and monstrous as it appears, in a cheerful spirit. This very attempt to blot out forever the hopes of an enslaved people may be one necessary link in the chain of events preparatory to the downfall and complete overthrow of the whole slave system.

The whole history of the antislavery movement is studded with proof that all measures devised and executed with a view to allay and diminish the antislavery agitation have only served to increase, intensify, and embolden that agitation. This wisdom of the crafty has been confounded, and the ungodly brought to nought. It was so with the Fugitive Slave Bill. It was so with the Kansas-Nebraska Bill; and it will be so with this last and most shocking of all pro-slavery devices, this Taney decision. . . .

—"A Speech of Frederick Douglass on the Dred Scott decision,"
Rochester, New York, 1857

39

IF THERE IS NO STRUGGLE, THERE IS NO PROGRESS

Despite the defeats and disappointments of the struggle against slavery and racism, Douglass continued to agitate for change. During a West Indies Emancipation

*Day celebration speech in Canandaigua, New York, on August 4, 1857, he con-
tended that revolutionary resistance to the rule of slavery was essential. "Who
would be free, themselves must strike the blow." He fought against apathy and
indifference, against the sense of powerlessness among his own people, whose causes
he well knew—poverty, discrimination, illiteracy, and the denial of human rights.
He saw them clearly and felt them sadly. Which is why, in this speech, he
underscores the lessons of those blacks anywhere in the world who had struck blows
for their own freedom.*

. . . THE WHOLE HISTORY OF THE PROGRESS OF HUMAN LIBERTY SHOWS THAT
all concessions yet made to her august claims have been born of earnest
struggle. The conflict has been exciting, agitating, all-absorbing, and for the
time being, putting all other tumults to silence. It must do this or it does
nothing. If there is no struggle there is no progress. Those who profess to
favor freedom and yet deprecate agitation are men who want crops without
plowing up the ground, they want rain without thunder and lightning. They
want the ocean without the awful roar of its many waters.

This struggle may be a moral one or it may be a physical one, and it may
be both moral and physical, but it must be a struggle. Power concedes nothing
without a demand. It never did and it never will. Find out just what any
people will quietly submit to, and you have found out the exact measure of
injustice and wrong which will be imposed upon them, and these will continue
till they are resisted with either words or blows, or with both. The limits of
tyrants are prescribed by the endurance of those whom they oppress. In the
light of these ideas, Negroes will be hunted at the North, and held and flogged
at the South, so long as they submit to those devilish outrages and make no
resistance, either moral or physical. Men may not get all they pay for in this
world, but they must certainly pay for all they get. If we ever get free from
the oppressions and wrongs heaped upon us, we must pay for their removal.
We must do this by labor, by suffering, by sacrifice, and if needs be, by our
lives and the lives of others.

Hence, my friends, every mother who, like Margaret Garner, plunges a
knife into the bosom of her infant to save it from the hell of our Christian
slavery should be held and honored as a benefactress. Every fugitive from
slavery who, like the noble William Thomas at Wilkesbarre, prefers to perish

in a river made red by his own blood to submission to the hellhounds who were hunting and shooting him should be esteemed as a glorious martyr, worthy to be held in grateful memory by our people. The fugitive Horace, at Mechanicsburgh, Ohio, the other day, who taught the slavecatchers from Kentucky that it was safer to arrest white men than to arrest him, did a most excellent service to our cause. Parker and his noble band of fifteen at Christiana, who defended themselves from the kidnappers with prayers and pistols, are entitled to the honor of making the first successful resistance to the Fugitive Slave Bill. But for that resistance, and the rescue of Jerry and Shadrack, the man-hunters would have hunted our hills and valleys here with the same freedom with which they now hunt their own dismal swamps.

There was an important lesson in the conduct of that noble Krooman in New York, the other day, who, supposing that the American Christians were about to enslave him, betook himself to the masthead and with knife in hand said he would cut his throat before he would be made a slave. Joseph Cinque on the deck of the *Amistad* did that which should make his name dear to us. He bore nature's burning protest against slavery. Madison Washington, who struck down his oppressor on the deck of the *Creole,* is more worthy to be remembered than the colored man who shot Pitcairn at Bunker Hill. . . .

This, then, is the truth concerning the inauguration of freedom in the British West Indies. Abolition was the act of the British government. The motive which led the government to act no doubt was mainly a philanthropic one, entitled to our highest admiration and gratitude. The national religion, the justice and humanity cried out in thunderous indignation against the foul abomination, and the government yielded to the storm. Nevertheless a share of the credit of the result falls justly to the slaves themselves. "Though slaves, they were rebellious slaves." They bore themselves well. They did not hug their chains but, according to their opportunities, swelled the general protest against oppression. What Wilberforce was endeavoring to win from the British Senate by his magic eloquence, the slaves themselves were endeavoring to gain by outbreaks and violence. The combined action of one and the other wrought out the final result. While one showed that slavery was wrong, the other showed that it was dangerous as well as wrong.

Mr. Wilberforce, peace man though he was and a model of piety, availed himself of this element to strengthen his case before the British Parliament and warned the British government of the danger of continuing slavery in the West Indies. There is no doubt that the fear of the consequences, acting with a sense of the moral evil of slavery, led to its abolition. The spirit of freedom was abroad in the island. Insurrection for freedom kept the planters in a constant state of alarm and trepidation. A standing army was necessary to keep the slaves in their chains. This state of facts could not be without weight in deciding the question of freedom in these countries. . . .

I am aware that the insurrectionary movements of the slaves were held by many to be prejudicial to their cause. This is said now of such movements at the South. The answer is that abolition followed close on the heels of insurrection in the West Indies, and Virginia was never nearer emancipation than when General Turner kindled the fires of insurrection at Southampton. . . .

—"The Significance of Emancipation in the West Indies:
An Address Delivered in Canandaigua, New York,
on August 4, 1857"

40

JOHN BROWN HAS STRUCK A MIGHTY BLOW

In mid-October 1859, sensational news of a raid by abolitionists on the federal arsenal at Harpers Ferry in Virginia (now West Virginia) was flashed to the nation. There was wild excitement over the attack by John Brown and his band of twenty-one men. Brown's aim was to take the town, distribute arms to the slaves in the vicinity, and spread a slave revolt across the South. The arsenal was taken, but the plan failed when federal troops crushed the revolt. Ten of Brown's men were killed, and Brown himself was wounded and made prisoner with the rest.

Douglass had openly endorsed violent resistance to slavery in recent years. He knew Brown well; the two had first met in 1848, when Douglass visited the Brown home in Springfield, Massachusetts. Brown loathed slaveholders and felt a bond with African-Americans trying to overthrow slavery. He had already conceived plans to that end. In 1856, while living in North Elba on a land grant from Gerrit Smith, Brown visited Douglass in Rochester. Again, in 1858, Brown discussed his plans with Douglass during a stay in his home. While Douglass did not reject his

plans, neither would he join them. Just before the raid on Harpers Ferry, Brown tried once more, during a meeting with Douglass at Chambersburg, Pennsylvania, to recruit him. But Douglass now believed Brown's plan was doomed to failure, and he refused to join him.

Douglass saw "moral greatness" in Brown's selfless dedication to racial equality and freedom. He was angered by the attempts of many to prove Brown was insane. Even friends of the antislavery movement were saying this in the hope of shielding Brown from Virginia's accusation of treason and to save him from a sentence of execution. In this essay Douglass upholds Brown, as did others such as Ralph Waldo Emerson, who said Brown was "a new saint, who will make the gallows glorious like the cross." The black poet Frances E. W. Harper wrote, "Already from your prison has come a shout of triumph against the giant sin of our country."

Brown was tried, convicted, and executed by hanging on December 2, 1859.

. . . Nor is it necessary to attribute Brown's deeds to the spirit of vengeance, invoked by the murder of his brave boys. That the barbarous cruelty from which he has suffered had its effect in intensifying his hatred of slavery is doubtless true. But his own statement, that he had been contemplating a bold strike for the freedom of the slaves for ten years, proves that he had resolved upon his present course long before he or his sons ever set foot in Kansas. His entire procedure in this matter disproves the charge that he was prompted by an impulse of mad revenge and shows that he was moved by the highest principles of philanthropy. His carefulness of the lives of unarmed persons—his humane and courteous treatment of his prisoners—his cool self-possession all through his trial—and especially his calm, dignified speech on receiving his sentence, all conspire to show that he was neither insane nor actuated by vengeful passion; and we hope that the country has heard the last of John Brown's madness.

The explanation of his conduct is perfectly natural and simple on its face. He believes the Declaration of Independence to be true and the Bible to be a guide to human conduct, and acting upon the doctrines of both, he threw himself against the serried ranks of American oppression and translated into heroic deeds the love of liberty and hatred of tyrants, with which he was inspired from both these forces acting upon his philanthropic and heroic soul.

This age is too gross and sensual to appreciate his deeds, and so calls him mad; but the future will write his epitaph upon the hearts of a people free from slavery because he struck the first effectual blow.

Not only is it true that Brown's whole movement proves him perfectly sane and free from merely revengeful passion, but he has struck the bottom line of the philosophy which underlies the abolition movement. He has attacked slavery with the weapons precisely adapted to bring it to the death. Moral considerations have long since been exhausted upon slaveholders. It is in vain to reason with them. One might as well hunt bears with ethics and political economy for weapons as to seek to "pluck the spoiled out of the hand of the oppressor" by the mere force of moral law. Slavery is a system of brute force. It shields itself behind might, rather than right. It must be met with its own weapons. Captain Brown has initiated a new mode of carrying on the crusade of freedom, and his blow has sent dread and terror throughout the entire ranks of the piratical army of slavery. His daring deeds may cost him his life, but priceless as is the value of that life, the blow he has struck will, in the end, prove to be worth its mighty cost. Like Samson, he has laid his hands upon the pillars of this great national temple of cruelty and blood, and when he falls, that temple will speedily crumble to its final doom, burying its denizens in its ruins.

—*Douglass' Monthly*, November 1859

41

FOR MR. LINCOLN

In May 1860, Abraham Lincoln was nominated for President by the Republican Party. The choice came on the third ballot, for Republicans were divided over Lincoln. Some thought him too inexperienced in politics; others thought he was too liberal to win. And there were other favorites, such as William Seward, the leading Republican in Douglass's own state of New York. But in his speeches, Lincoln had demonstrated that the Founding Fathers had exercised their constitutional right in excluding slavery from the territories. And he saw slavery as a moral issue: "If slavery is right," he had said in his recent Cooper Union speech, "all words, acts, laws, and constitutions against it are themselves wrong, and should be silenced and swept away. . . . Let us have faith that right makes might, and in that faith, let us, to the end, dare to do our duty as we understand it."

So Douglass supported him, hoping Lincoln would live up to his own principles.

MR. LINCOLN IS A MAN OF UNBLEMISHED PRIVATE CHARACTER; A LAWYER, standing near the front rank at the bar of his own state, has a cool, well-balanced head; great firmness of will; is perseveringly industrious; and one of the most frank, honest men in political life. He cannot lay claim to any literary culture beyond the circle of his practical duties, or to any of the graces found at courts or in diplomatic circles, but must rely upon his "good hard sense" and honesty of purpose as capital for the campaign and the qualities to give character to his administration. His friends cannot as yet claim for him a place in the front rank of statesmanship, whatever may be their faith in his latent capacities. His political life is thus far to his credit, but it is a political life of fair promise rather than one of rich fruitage.

It was, perhaps, this fact that obtained for him the nomination. Our political history has often illustrated the truth that a man may be too great a statesman to become President. . . .

If, therefore, Mr. Lincoln possesses great capacities and is yet to be proved a great statesman, it is lucky for him that a political exigency moved his party to take him on trust and before his greatness was ripe, or he would have lost the chance. But when once elected, it will be no longer dangerous for him to develop great qualities, and we hope that in taking him on a "profession of his faith" rather than on the recommendations of his political life, his party will witness his continual "growth in grace," and his administration will redound to the glory of his country and his own fame.

As to his principles, there is no reason why the friends of Mr. Seward should not heartily support him. He is a radical Republican and is fully committed to the doctrine of the "irrepressible conflict." In his debates with Douglas, he came fully up to the highest mark of Republicanism, and he is a man of will and nerve and will not back down from his own assertions.

—*Douglass' Monthly,* June 1860

42

WHAT THE REPUBLICANS SHOULD DO

As the election campaign progressed, Douglass reviewed its progress with an acute concern for what the Republican Party was saying and doing, or failing to say and do. In a speech on August 1, 1860, he challenged the Republican Party to use the power victory would give it to act against the vicious law that restricted not only African-Americans but the liberties of all people.

. . . IF THE REPUBLICAN PARTY SHALL ARREST THE SPREAD OF SLAVERY; IF IT shall exclude from office all such in the slave states who know only slavery as master and lawgiver, who burn every newspaper and letter supposed to contain antislavery matter, who refuse to hand a black man a letter from the Post Office because he is of the hated color, and will put men into office who will administer them justly and impartially; if it will send ministers and other agents to foreign courts, who will represent other interests than slavery, and will give a colored citizen of a free state a passport as any other citizen— place the honor of the nation on the side of freedom, encourage freedom of speech and of the press, protect Republican principles and organizations in the slave states—that party, though it may not abolish slavery, will not have existed in vain.

But if, on the other hand, it shall seek first of all to make itself acceptable to slaveholders—do what it can to efface all traces of its antislavery origin, fall to slave-catching, swear by the Dred Scott decision, and perpetuate slavery in the District of Columbia—it will disappoint the hopes of all its heart friends and will be deserted, shunned, and abhorred as the other parties now are, and its place will be taken by another and better party, organized on higher ground and animated by a nobler spirit. Bad as the moral condition of this country is, and powerful as may be the influence of prejudice, the sun of science and civilization has risen too high in the heavens for any party to stand long on the mean, narrow, and selfish idea of a "white man's party." This is an age of universal ideas. Men are men, and governments cannot afford much longer to make discriminations between men in regard to personal liberty. Surely the

Republican Party will not fall into the mistake or the crime of competing with the old parties in the old wornout business of feeding popular malignity by acts of discrimination against the free colored people of the United States. I certainly look to that party for a nobler policy than that avowed by some connected with the Republican organization.

—*Douglass' Monthly*, October 1860

43

THE BENEFITS OF LINCOLN'S VICTORY

With November 1860, came the victory of Lincoln and cries of "secession," "disunion," and "Southern Confederacy" from the defeated slave states of the South. Douglass evaluated the significance of the Republican campaign and of Lincoln's election, placing them against the history of the past fifty years when the slaveholders had dominated national politics and policy.

. . . WHAT, THEN, HAS BEEN GAINED TO THE ANTISLAVERY CAUSE BY THE election of Mr. Lincoln? Not much, in itself considered, but very much when viewed in the light of its relations and bearings. For fifty years the country has taken the law from the lips of an exacting, haughty, and imperious slave oligarchy. The masters of slaves have been masters of the Republic. Their authority was almost undisputed, and their power irresistible. They were the President makers of the Republic, and no aspirant dared to hope for success against their frown. Lincoln's election has vitiated their authority and broken their power. It has taught the North its strength and shown the South its weakness. More important still, it has demonstrated the possibility of electing, if not an abolitionist, at least an antislavery reputation to the Presidency of the United States. The years are few since it was thought possible that the Northern people could be wrought up to the exercise of such startling courage. Hitherto the threat of disunion has been as potent over the politicians of the North as the cat-o'-nine-tails is over the backs of the slaves. Mr. Lincoln's election breaks this enchantment, dispels this terrible nightmare, and awakes the nation to the consciousness of new powers and the possibility of a higher destiny than the perpetual bondage to an ignoble fear.

Another probable effect will be to extinguish the reviving fires of the accursed foreign slave trade, which for a year or two have been kindled all along the Southern coast of the Union. The Republican Party is under no necessity to pass laws on this subject. It has only to enforce and execute the laws already on the statute book. The moral influence of such prompt, complete, and unflinching execution of the laws will be great, not only in arresting the specific evil but in arresting the tide of popular demoralization with which the successful prosecution of the horrid trade in naked men and women was overspreading the country. To this duty the Republican Party will be prompted, not only by the conscience of the North but by what perhaps will be more controlling party interests.

It may also be conceded that the election of Lincoln and Hamlin, notwithstanding the admission of the former that the South is entitled to an efficient Fugitive Slave Law, will render the practice of recapturing and returning to slavery persons who have heroically succeeded, or may hereafter succeed in reaching the free states, more unpopular and odious than it would have been had either Douglas, Bell, or Breckinridge been elected. Slaves may yet be hunted, caught, and carried back to slavery, but the number will be greatly diminished because of the popular disinclination to execute the cruel and merciless Fugitive Slave Law. Had Lincoln been defeated, the fact would have been construed by slaveholders and their guilty minions of the country as strong evidence of the soundness of the North in respect to the alleged duty of hounding down and handing over the panting fugitive to the vengeance of his infuriated master. No argument is needed to prove this gain to the side of freedom.

But chief among the benefits of the election has been the canvass itself. . . . The canvass has sent all over the North most learned and eloquent men to utter the great truths which abolitionists have for twenty years been earnestly but unsuccessfully endeavoring to get before the public mind and conscience. We may rejoice in the dissemination of the truth by whomsoever proclaimed, for the truth will bear its own weight and bring forth its own fruit. . . .

—*Douglass' Monthly*, December 1860

44

HE MUST DO THIS, OR WORSE

Just before Lincoln took his oath of office and delivered his First Inaugural Address, Douglass set down what his hopes were for the new administration's policy.

WILL HE CALL UPON THE HAUGHTY SLAVE MASTERS, WHO HAVE RISEN IN ARMS to break up the government, to lay down those arms and return to loyalty, or meet the doom of traitors and rebels? He must do this, or do worse. He must do this, or consent to be the despised representative of a defied and humbled government. He must do this, or own that party platforms are the merest devices of scheming politicians to cheat the people, and to enable them to crawl up to place and power. He must do this, or compromise the fundamental principle upon which he was elected, to wit, the right and duty of Congress to prohibit the further extension of slavery.

Will he compromise? Time and events will soon answer this question. For the present, there is much reason to believe that he will not consent to any compromise which will violate the principle upon which he was elected; and since none which does not utterly trample upon that principle can be accepted by the South, we have a double assurance that there will be no compromise, and that the contest must now be decided, and decided forever, which of the two, Freedom or Slavery, shall give law to this Republic. Let the conflict come, and God speed the right, must be the wish of every true-hearted American, as well as of that of an onlooking world.

—*Douglass' Monthly*, March 1861

THE WAR YEARS

THE WAR YEARS WERE A DECISIVE ERA IN HISTORY—FOR ALL AMERIcans, black and white; for the Union; and for the world. The Civil War began with the federal government proclaiming that its only object was to preserve the Union. But as tens of thousands died on the battlefield, more and more people in the North came to believe that slavery had been the primary cause of the conflict. And that if victory was to be won, and the Union saved, then slavery must be ended.

Such great changes in mass thinking do not come about by chance. They are the result of events, true, but those events need to be understood. The lessons of history must be explained if people are to grasp their meaning and to act upon it. This is where Frederick Douglass made a great contribution. He educated the public—in the articles, editorials, and letters he wrote, in the speeches he gave, in the meetings he held. Where others were uncertain, hesitant, unsure of what should be done next, Douglass grasped the revolutionary nature of the war. Again and again he insisted that the war must end with the destruction of human bondage and the shattering of the slaveholders' power. To that end, he argued, the African-Americans must be armed and allowed to fight for the abolition of slavery.

In time this became the policy of the Lincoln administration. The man who twenty years before had been a slave used the talents he had developed to help bring about the liberation of his people.

45

THE GREAT MISTAKE

With the firing on Fort Sumter by the Confederates on April 12, 1861, the Civil War began. Lincoln declared that "insurrection" existed and called for seventy-

five thousand three-month volunteers to put it down. Douglass almost at once called for the use of African-American troops. In this talk given at Zion Church in Rochester, on June 30, he voiced a demand he would continue making for the next two years. If the Union forces were to win the war: free the slaves.

THE GREAT AND GRAND MISTAKE OF THE CONDUCT OF THE WAR THUS FAR IS the attitude of our army and government toward slavery. That attitude deprives us of the moral support of the world. It degrades the war into a war of sections and robs it of the dignity of being a mighty effort of a great people to vanquish and destroy a huge system of cruelty and barbarism. It gives to the contest the appearance of a struggle for power, rather than a struggle for the advancement and disenthrallment of a nation. It cools the ardor of our troops and disappoints the hopes of the friends of humanity.

Now, evade and equivocate as we may, slavery is not only the cause of the beginning of this war, but slavery is the sole support of the rebel cause. It is, so to speak, the very stomach of this rebellion.

The war is called a sectional war; but there is nothing in the sections, in the difference of climate or soil, to produce conflicts between the two sections. It is not a quarrel between cotton and corn—between live oak and livestock. The two sections are inhabited by the same people. They speak the same language and are naturally united. There is nothing existing between them to prevent national concord and enjoyment of the profoundest peace but the existence of slavery. That is the fly in our pot of ointment—the disturbing force in our social system. Everybody knows this, everybody feels this, and yet the great mass of the people refuse to confess it, and the government refuses to recognize it. We talk the irrepressible conflict and practically give the lie to our talk. We wage war against slaveholding rebels and yet protect and augment the motive which has moved the slaveholders to rebellion. We strike at the effect, and leave the cause unharmed. Fire will not burn it out of us—water cannot wash it out of us—that this war with the slaveholders can never be brought to a desirable termination until slavery, the guilty cause of all our national troubles, has been totally and forever abolished.

—*Douglass' Monthly*, August 1861

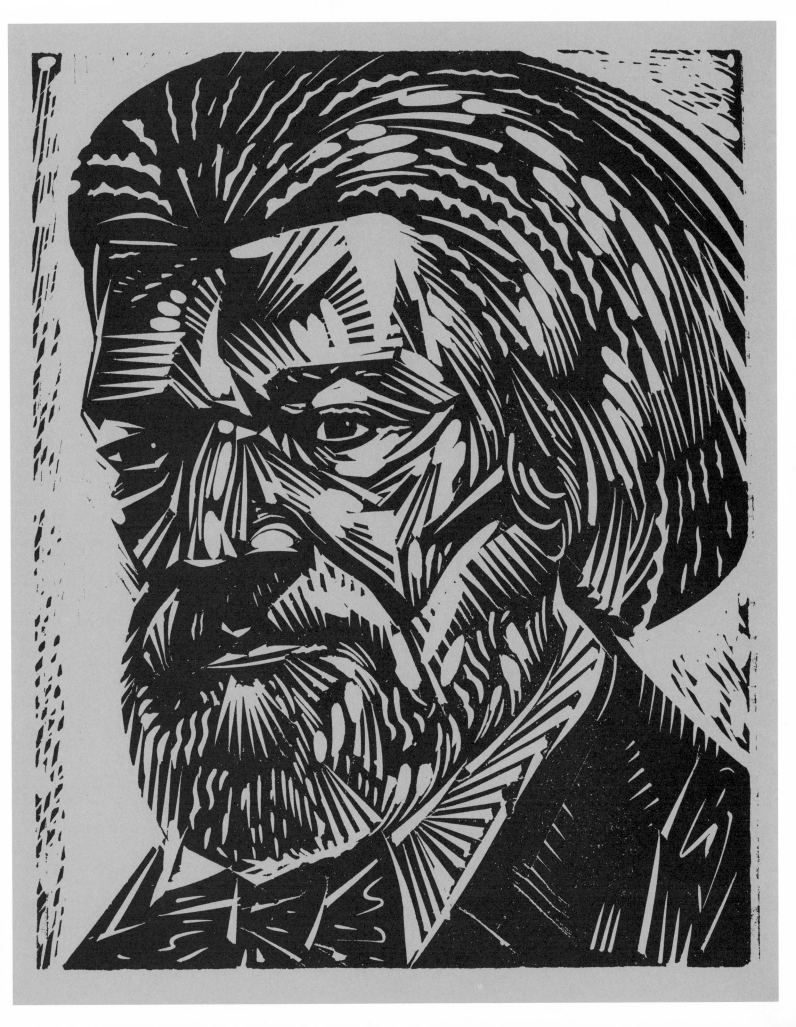

46

FIGHTING REBELS WITH ONLY ONE HAND

In the early stages of the war, Douglass observed bitterly that Lincoln's government was trying to put down the slaveholders' rebellion while at the same time protecting and preserving slavery. As Confederate victories threatened even Washington, Douglass demanded that the president stop giving in to prejudice and allow black men to join the fight.

WHAT UPON EARTH IS THE MATTER WITH THE AMERICAN GOVERNMENT AND people? Do they really covet the world's ridicule as well as their own social and political ruin? What are they thinking about, or don't they condescend to think at all? So indeed it would seem from their blindness in dealing with the tremendous issue now upon them. Was there ever anything like it before? They are sorely pressed on every hand by a vast army of slaveholding rebels, flushed with success, and infuriated by the darkest inspirations of a deadly hate, bound to rule or ruin. Washington, the seat of government, after ten thousand assurances to the contrary, is now positively in danger of falling before the rebel army. Maryland, a little while ago considered safe for the Union, is now admitted to be studded with the materials for insurrection, which may flame forth at any moment.

Every resource of the nation, whether of men or money, whether of wisdom or strength, could be well employed to avert the impending ruin. Yet most evidently the demands of the hour are not comprehended by the cabinet or the crowd. Our president, governors, generals, and secretaries are calling with almost frantic vehemence for men. "Men! Men! Send us men!" they scream, or the cause of the Union is gone, the life of a great nation is ruthlessly sacrificed, and the hopes of a great nation go out in darkness; and yet these very officers, representing the people and government, steadily and persistently refuse to receive the very class of men which have a deeper interest in the defeat and humiliation of the rebels than all others.

Men are wanted in Missouri, wanted in Western Virginia, to hold and defend what has been already gained; they are wanted in Texas, and all along the seacoast, and though the government has at its command a class in the country deeply interested in suppressing the insurrection, it sternly refuses to summon from among the vast multitude a single man, and degrades and insults the whole class by refusing to allow any of their number to defend with their strong arms and brave hearts the national cause. What a spectacle of blind, unreasoning prejudice and pusillanimity is this! The national edifice is on fire. Every man who can carry a bucket of water or remove a brick is wanted; but those who have the care of the building, having a profound respect for the feeling of the national burglars who set the building on fire, are determined that the flames shall only be extinguished by Indo-Caucasian hands, and to have the building burnt rather than save it by means of any other. Such is the pride, the stupid prejudice, and folly that rules the hour.

Why does the government reject the Negro? Is he not a man? Can he not wield a sword, fire a gun, march and countermarch, and obey orders like any other? Is there the least reason to believe that a regiment of well-drilled Negroes would deport themselves less soldierlike on the battlefield than the raw troops gathered up generally from the towns and cities of the State of New York? We do believe that such soldiers, if allowed now to take up arms in defense of the government and made to feel that they are hereafter to be recognized as persons having rights, would set the highest example of order and general good behavior to their fellow soldiers and in every way add to the national power.

If persons so humble as we can be allowed to speak to the President of the United States, we should ask him if this dark and terrible hour of the nation's extremity is a time for consulting a mere vulgar and unnatural prejudice. We should ask him if national preservation and necessity were not better guides in this emergency than either the tastes of the rebels or the pride and prejudices of the vulgar. We would tell him that General Jackson in a slave state fought side by side with Negroes at New Orleans, and like a true man, despising meanness, he bore testimony to their bravery at the close of the war. We would tell him that colored men in Rhode Island and Connecticut performed their full share in the war of the Revolution, and that men of the same color, such as the noble Shields Green, Nathaniel Turner, and Denmark Vesey stand ready to peril everything at the command of the government.

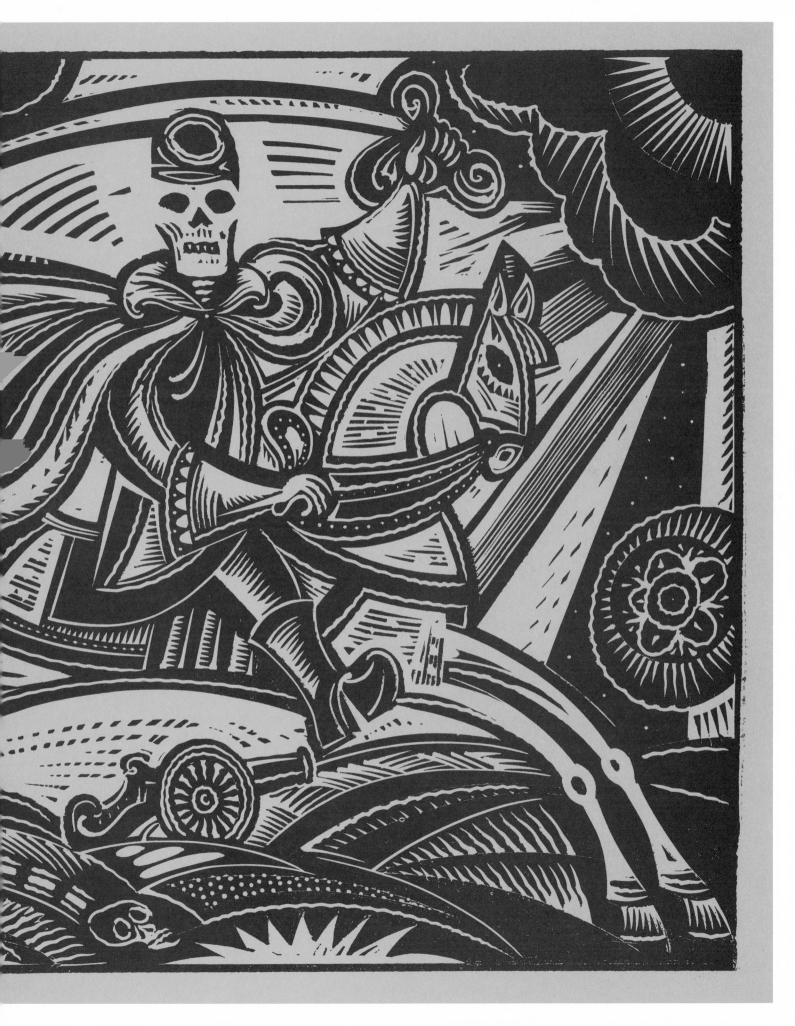

We would tell him that this is no time to fight with one hand when both are needed; that this is no time to fight only with your white hand and allow your black hand to remain tied. . . .

—*Douglass' Monthly*, September 1861

47

JUST LET THEM ALONE

Even before the defeat of the South seemed a likely prospect, racial prejudice exhibited itself in the North as people worried about what freed slaves might do. All sorts of fears came to light: they'd slit their masters' throats, they'd become vagrants, they'd come North and refuse to work, they'd undercut workers' wages, they'd end up paupers or criminals and a burden on the state. . . . To the question what shall be done with the slaves if emancipated, Douglass gave this answer early in 1862.

OUR ANSWER IS, DO NOTHING WITH THEM; MIND YOUR BUSINESS, AND LET THEM mind theirs. Your doing with them is their great misfortune. They have been undone by your doings, and all they now ask, and really have need of at your hands, is just to let them alone. They suffer by every interference and succeed best by being let alone. The Negro should have been let alone in Africa—let alone when the pirates and robbers offered him for sale in our Christian slave markets (more cruel and inhuman than the Mohammedan slave markets)—let alone by courts, judges, politicians, legislators, and slave drivers—let alone altogether, and assured that they were thus to be let alone forever, and that they must now make their own way in the world, just the same as any and every other variety of the human family. As colored men, we only ask to be allowed to do with ourselves, subject only to the same great laws for the welfare of human society which apply to other men—Jews, Gentiles, Barbarian, Scythian. Let us stand upon our own legs, work with our own hands, and eat bread in the sweat of our own brows.

When you, our white fellow countrymen, have attempted to do anything for us, it has generally been to deprive us of some right, power, or privilege which you yourself would die before you would submit to have taken from you. When the planters of the West Indies used to attempt to puzzle the pure-minded Wilberforce with the question, How shall we get rid of slavery? his simple answer was "quit stealing." In like manner, we answer those who are perpetually puzzling their brains with questions as what shall be done with the Negro, "let him alone and mind your own business." If you see him plowing in the open field, leveling the forest, at work with a spade, a rake, a hoe, a pickax, or a bill—let him alone; he has a right to work. If you see him on his way to school, with spelling book, geography, and arithmetic in his hands—let him alone. Don't shut the door in his face nor bolt your gates against him; he has a right to learn—let him alone. Don't pass laws to degrade him. If he has a ballot in his hand and is on his way to the ballot box to deposit his vote for the man whom he thinks will most justly and wisely administer the government which has the power of life and death over him as well as others—let him alone; his right of choice as much deserves respect and protection as your own. If you see him on his way to the church, exercising religious liberty in accordance with this or that religious persuasion—let him alone. Don't meddle with him, nor trouble yourselves with any questions as to what shall be done with him. . . .

What shall be done with the Negro if emancipated? Deal justly with him. He is a human being, capable of judging between good and evil, right and wrong, liberty and slavery, and is as much a subject of law as any other man; therefore, deal justly with him. He is, like other men, sensible of the motives of reward and punishment. Give him wages for his work, and let hunger pinch him if he doesn't work. He knows the difference between fullness and famine, plenty and scarcity. "But will he work?" Why should he not? He is used to it. His hands are already hardened by toil, and he has no dreams of ever getting a living by any other means than by hard work. But would you turn them all loose? Certainly! We are no better than our Creator. He has turned them loose, and why should not we?

But would you let them all stay here? Why not? What better is here than there? Will they occupy more room as freemen than as slaves? Is the presence of a black freeman less agreeable than that of a black slave? Is an object of your injustice and cruelty a more ungrateful sight than one of your justice and benevolence? You have borne the one more than two hundred years—can't you bear the other long enough to try the experiment?

"But would it be safe?" No good reason can be given why it would not be. There is much more reason for apprehension from slavery than from freedom. Slavery provokes and justifies incendiarism, murder, robbery, assassination, and all manner of violence. But why not let them go off by themselves? That is a matter we would leave exclusively to themselves. Besides, when you, the American people, shall once do justice to the enslaved colored people, you will not want to get rid of them. Take away the motive which slavery supplies for getting rid of the free black people of the South and there is not a single state, from Maryland to Texas, which would desire to be rid of its black people. Even with the obvious disadvantage to slavery, which such contact is, there is scarcely a slave state which could be carried for the unqualified expulsion of the free colored people. Efforts at such expulsion have been made in Maryland, Virginia, and South Carolina, and all have failed, just because the black man as a freeman is a useful member of society. To drive him away, and thus deprive the South of his labor, would be as absurd and monstrous as for a man to cut off his right arm, the better to enable himself to work.

—*Douglass' Monthly*, January 1862

48

HARSH WORDS

With the Union and Confederate forces fighting in central Virginia and the war soon to move into Maryland, Lincoln met with a delegation of five blacks at the White House on August 14, 1862. It was the first formal meeting of any president with African-Americans. The tone was friendly, but Lincoln's expression of support for schemes to rid the country of blacks by colonizing them abroad caused angry protest by blacks.

Douglass, in his monthly paper, accused Lincoln of "pride of race and blood . . . contempt for Negroes . . . and canting hypocrisy." He wondered how an honest man could come to such views. This would be the harshest criticism he ever made of Lincoln.

. . . THE ARGUMENT OF MR. LINCOLN IS THAT THE DIFFERENCE BETWEEN THE white and black races renders it impossible for them to live together in the same country without detriment to both. Colonization, therefore, he holds to be in the duty and the interest of the colored people. Mr. Lincoln takes care in urging his colonization scheme to furnish a weapon to all the ignorant and base, who need only the countenance of men in authority to commit all kinds of violence and outrage upon the colored people of the country. Taking advantage of his position and of the prevailing prejudice against them, he affirms that their presence in the country is the real first cause of the war, and logically enough, if the premises were sound, assumes the necessity of their removal.

It does not require any great amount of skill to point out the fallacy and expose the unfairness of the assumption, for by this time every man who has an ounce of brain in his head, no matter to which party he may belong, and even Mr. Lincoln himself, must know quite well that the mere presence of the colored race never could have provoked this horrid and desolating rebellion. Mr. Lincoln knows that in Mexico, Central America, and South America, many distinct races live peaceably together in the enjoyment of equal rights, and that the civil wars which occasionally disturb the peace of those regions never originated in the difference of the races inhabiting them. A horse thief pleading that the existence of the horse is the apology for his theft or a highwayman contending that the money in the traveler's pocket is the sole first cause of his robbery are about as much entitled to respect as is the president's reasoning at this point.

No, Mr. President, it is not the innocent horse that makes the horse thief, not the traveler's purse that makes the highway robber, and it is not the presence of the Negro that causes this foul and unnatural war, but the cruel and brutal cupidity of those who wish to possess horses, money, and Negroes by means of theft, robbery, and rebellion. Mr. Lincoln further knows, or ought to know at least, that Negro hatred and prejudice of color are neither original nor invincible vices, but merely the offshoots of that root of all crimes and evils—slavery. If the colored people, instead of having been stolen and forcibly brought to the United States, had come as free immigrants, like the German and the Irish, never thought of as suitable objects of property, they never would have become the objects of aversion and bitter persecution, nor would there ever have been divulged and propagated the arrogant and malignant nonsense about natural repellancy and the incompatibility of races. . . .

—*Douglass' Monthly*, September 1862

49

A GLORIOUS ERA HAS BEGUN

On January 1, 1863, Lincoln issued the Emancipation Proclamation. He made the decision as the tide of war began at last to turn in the Union's favor. Up to now he had delayed doing what black leaders had demanded of him all along, for he knew racism was rampant in the North and that few soldiers wanted to die to free the slaves. But in recent months, public feeling had begun to change, and Lincoln used his presidential war power as the one quick way to end slavery.

Douglass hailed the proclamation as a great moral act and the beginning of a new and glorious era in American history.

. . . BORN AND REARED AS A SLAVE, AS I WAS, AND WEARING ON MY BACK THE marks of the slave driver's lash, as I do, it is natural that I should value the Emancipation Proclamation for what it is destined to do for the slaves. I do value it for that. It is a mighty event for the bondman, but it is a still mightier event for the nation at large; and mighty as it is for both, the slave and the nation, it is still mightier when viewed in its relation to the cause of truth and justice throughout the world. It is in this last character that I prefer to consider it.

There are certain great national acts which, by their relation to universal principles, properly belong to the whole human family, and Abraham Lincoln's proclamation of the first of January, 1863, is one of these acts. Henceforth that day shall take rank with the Fourth of July. Henceforth it becomes the date of a new and glorious era in the history of American liberty. Henceforth it shall stand associated in the minds of men with all those stately steps of mankind, from the regions of error and oppression, which have lifted them from the trial by poison and fire to the trial by jury, from the arbitrary will of a despot to the sacred writ of habeas corpus, from abject serfdom to absolute citizenship.

It will stand in the history of civilization with Catholic Emancipation, with the British Reform Bill, with the repeal of Corn Laws, and with that noble act of Russian liberty by which twenty millions of serfs, against the clamors of haughty tyrants, have been released from servitude. Aye! It will stand with every distinguished event which marks any advance made by mankind from the thralldom and darkness of error to the glorious liberty of truth; I believe in the millenium—the final perfection of the race—and hail this proclamation, though wrung out under the goading lash of a stern military necessity, as one reason of the hope that is in me. Men may see in it only a military necessity. To me it has a higher significance. It is a grand moral necessity. . . .

—*Douglass' Monthly*, March 1863

50

MEN OF COLOR, TO ARMS!

At the roar of the first cannon, the abolitionists had tried to convince Lincoln and the North that the Union cause would not triumph unless the war was fought to end its cause—slavery. Douglass kept pressing the government to enlist both free blacks and slaves to fight in an army of liberation. Finally, after the Emancipation Proclamation, Lincoln opened the Union forces to African-Americans.

In a broadside he published on March 21, 1863, Douglass issued a flaming call to arms. His own sons, Lewis and Charles, were among the first to respond. By the war's end, 180,000 blacks had served in the Union army (140,000 of them ex-slaves), and 30,000 in the navy. Another 250,000 had helped the military as laborers.

WHEN FIRST THE REBEL CANNON SHATTERED THE WALLS OF SUMTER AND DROVE away its starving garrison, I predicted that the war, then and there inaugurated, would not be fought out entirely by white men. Every month's experience during these weary years has confirmed that opinion. A war undertaken

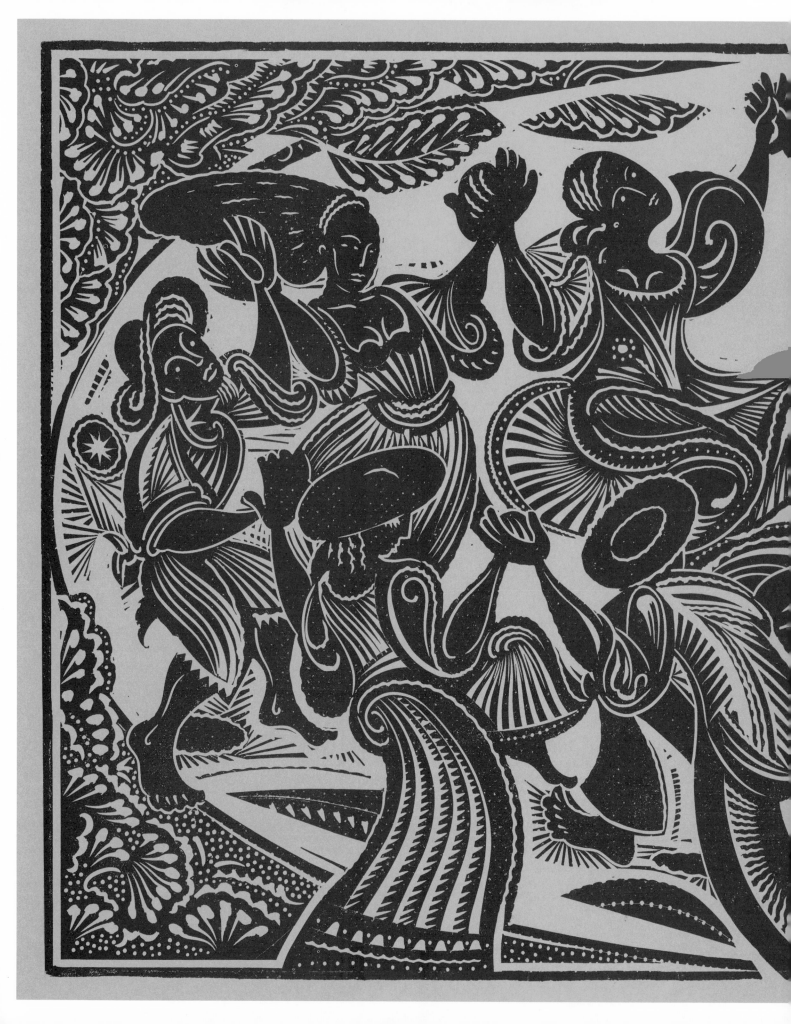

and brazenly carried on for the perpetual enslavement of colored men calls logically and loudly for colored men to help suppress it. Only a moderate share of sagacity was needed to see that the arm of the slave was the best defense against the arm of the slaveholder. Hence with every reverse to the national arms, with every exulting shout of victory raised by the slaveholding rebels, I have implored the imperiled nation to unchain against her foes her powerful black hand.

Slowly and reluctantly that appeal is beginning to be heeded. Stop not now to complain that it was not heeded sooner. . . .

By every consideration which binds you to your enslaved fellow country-men and the peace and welfare of your country; by every aspiration which you cherish for the freedom and equality of yourselves and your children; by all the ties of blood and identity which make us one with the brave black men now fighting our battles in Louisiana and in South Carolina, I urge you to fly to arms and smite with death the power that would bury the government and your liberty in the same hopeless grave.

I wish I could tell you that the State of New York calls you to this high honor. For the moment her constituted authorities are silent on the subject. They will speak by and by, and doubtless on the right side, but we are not compelled to wait for her. We can get at the throat of treason and slavery through the State of Massachusetts. She was first in the War of Independence; first to break the chains of her slaves; first to make the black man equal before the law; first to admit colored children to her common schools; and she was first to answer with her blood the alarm cry of the nation when its capital was menaced by rebels. You know her patriotic governor, and you know Charles Sumner. I need not add more.

Massachusetts now welcomes you to arms as soldiers. She has but a small colored population from which to recruit. She has full leave of the general government to send one regiment to the war, and she has undertaken to do it. Go quickly and help fill up the first colored regiment from the North. I am authorized to assure you that you will receive the same wages, the same rations, the same equipment, the same protection, the same treatment, and the same bounty secured to the white soldiers. You will be led by able and skillful officers, men who will take especial pride in your efficiency and success. They will be quick to accord to you all the honor you shall merit by your valor and see that your rights and feelings are respected by other soldiers. I have assured myself on these points and can speak with authority.

More than twenty years of unswerving devotion to our common cause may give me some humble claim to be trusted at this momentous crisis. I will not argue. To do so implies hesitation and doubt, and you do not hesitate. You do not doubt. The day dawns; the morning star is bright upon the horizon! The iron gate of our prison stands half open. One gallant rush from the North will fling it wide open, while four millions of our brothers and sisters shall march out into liberty. The chance is now given you to end in a day the bondage of centuries and to rise in one bound from social degradation to the plane of common equality with all other varieties of men.

Remember Denmark Vesey of Charleston; remember Nathaniel Turner of Southampton; remember Shields Green and Copeland, who followed noble John Brown and fell as glorious martyrs for the cause of the slave. Remember that in a contest with oppression the Almighty has no attribute which can take sides with oppressors.

The case is before you. This is our golden opportunity. Let us accept it and forever wipe out the dark reproaches unsparingly hurled against us by our enemies. Let us win for ourselves the gratitude of our country and the best blessings of our posterity through all time.

—"Broadside," Rochester, New York, March 21, 1863

51

YOUR BEST DEFENDER

In Lincoln's Gettysburg Address, given on November 19, 1863, at the dedication of the soldiers' cemetery on the site of the great battle, he had spoken of "a new birth of freedom" needed by the nation if it was to survive. Two weeks later, Douglass gave a similar message at the thirtieth anniversary celebration of the birth of the American Anti-Slavery Society. Now we are fighting for a new Union, he said, one in which there would be "no North, no South . . . no black, no white, but a solidarity of nation, making every slave free, and every free man a voter." He went on to explain why it was vital to give black men the vote and to elect them to Congress.

. . . MR. PRESIDENT, I HAVE A PATRIOTIC ARGUMENT IN FAVOR OF INSISTING upon the immediate enfranchisement of the slaves of the South; and it is this: When this rebellion shall have been put down, when the arms shall have fallen from the guilty hands of traitors, you will need the friendship of the slaves of the South, of those millions there. Four or five million men are not of inconsiderable importance at any time; but they will be doubly important when you come to reorganize and reestablish republican institutions in the South. Will you mock those bondmen by breaking their chains with one hand, and with the other giving their rebel masters the elective franchise and robbing them of theirs? I tell you, the Negro is your friend. You will make him your friend by emancipating him. But you will make him not only your friend in sentiment and heart by enfranchising him, but you will make him your best defender, your best protector against the traitors and the descendants of those traitors, who will inherit the hate, the bitter revenge which will crystalize all over the South and seek to circumvent the government that they could not throw off.

You will need the black man there, as a watchman and patrol; and you may need him as a soldier. You may need him to uphold in peace, as he is now upholding in war, the star-spangled banner. . . .

Let the Negro have a vote. It will be helping him from the jaws of the wolf. We are surrounded by those that, like the wolf, will use their jaws if you give the elective franchise to the descendants of the traitors and keep it from the black man. We ought to be voters there. We ought to be members of Congress. You may as well make up your minds that you have got to see something dark down that way. There is no way to get rid of it. I am a candidate already!

—Proceedings of the American Anti-Slavery Society at its Third Decade, Held in the City of Philadelphia, December 3–4, 1863

52

A BLACK MAN AT THE WHITE HOUSE

At that same December meeting of the abolitionists in Philadelphia, Douglass told his audience of his meeting in late July with "Honest Abe" in the White House.

It was his first conversation with the president, and he obviously enjoyed not only the great event but the telling of it. Douglass was not completely satisfied with Lincoln's response to his demands that racial discrimination in the services be ended and that black soldiers be given equal treatment in every respect. But he was much impressed by Lincoln's frank and respectful responses and believed that he would continue to move in the right direction.

. . . PERHAPS YOU MAY LIKE TO KNOW HOW THE PRESIDENT OF THE UNITED States received a black man at the White House. I will tell you how he received me—just as you have seen one gentleman receive another; with a hand and a voice well balanced between a kind cordiality and a respectful reserve. I tell you I felt big there! Let me tell you how I got to him; because everybody can't get to him. He has to be a little guarded in admitting spectators. The manner of getting to him gave me an idea that the cause was rolling on. The stairway was crowded with applicants. Some of them looked eager; and I have no doubt some of them had a purpose in being there and wanted to see the president for the good of the country! They were white; and as I was the only dark spot among them, I expected to have to wait at least half a day—I had heard of men waiting a week—but in two minutes after I sent in my card, the messenger came out and respectfully invited "Mr. Douglass" in. I could hear in the eager multitude outside, as they saw me pressing and elbowing my way through, the remark, "Yes, damn it, I knew they would let the n———r through," in a kind of despairing voice—a Peace Democrat, I suppose.

When I went in, the president was sitting in his usual position, I was told, with his feet in different parts of the room, taking it easy. . . . As I came in and approached him, the president began to rise, and he continued rising until he stood over me, and, reaching out his hand, he said, "Mr. Douglass, I know you; I have read about you, and Mr. Seward has told me about you"; putting me quite at ease at once.

Now, you will want to know how I was impressed by him. I will tell you that, too. He impressed me as being just what every one of you have been in the habit of calling him—an honest man. I never met with a man, who, on the first blush, impressed me more entirely with his sincerity, with his devotion to his country, and with his determination to save it at all hazards.

He told me (I think he did me more honor than I deserve) that I had made a little speech, somewhere in New York, and it had got into the papers, and among the things I had said was this: That if I were called upon to state what I regarded as the most sad and most disheartening feature in our present political and military situation, it would not be the various disasters experienced by our armies and our navies on flood and field, but it would be the tardy, hesitating, vacillating policy of the president of the United States; and the president said to me, "Mr. Douglass, I have been charged with being tardy, and the like"; and he went on and partly admitted that he might seem slow; but he said, "I am charged with vacillating; but, Mr. Douglass, I do not think that charge can be sustained; I think it cannot be shown that when I have once taken a position, I have ever retreated from it."

That I regarded as the most significant point in what he said during our interview. I told him that he had been somewhat slow in proclaiming equal protection to our colored soldiers and prisoners; and he said that the country needed talking up to that point. He hesitated in regard to it, when he felt that the country was not ready for it. He knew that the colored man throughout this country was a despised man, a hated man, and that if he at first came out with such a proclamation, all the hatred which is poured on the head of the Negro race would be visited on his administration. He said that there was preparatory work needed, and that that preparatory work had now been done. And he said, "Remember this, Mr. Douglass; remember that Milliken's Bend, Port Hudson, and Fort Wagner are recent events; and that these were necessary to prepare the way for this very proclamation of mine." I thought it was reasonable, but came to the conclusion that while Abraham Lincoln will not go down to posterity as Abraham the Great, or as Abraham the Wise, or as Abraham the Eloquent—although he is all three: wise, great, and eloquent—he will go down to posterity, if the country is saved, as Honest Abraham, and going down thus, his name may be written anywhere in this wide world of ours side by side with that of Washington, without disparaging the latter. . . .

—*Proceedings of the American Anti-Slavery Society at its*
Third Decade, Held in the City of Philadelphia,
December 3–4, 1863

53

WE WANT A COUNTRY . . .

What the Civil War meant to Douglass he set forth in a speech called "The Mission of the War." In the winter of 1863–64, he outlined his hopes and his program to many audiences on the lecture circuit. His ideas about a new country to be built on the ashes of the old foreshadowed what the radical Republicans would try to achieve through their plan for Reconstruction.

. . . WHAT BUSINESS HAVE WE TO BE POURING OUT OUR TREASURE AND SHEDding our best blood like water for that old worn-out, dead and buried Union, which had already become a calamity and a curse? The fact is, we are not fighting for any such thing, and we ought to come out under our own true colors and let the South and the whole world know that we don't want and will not have anything analogous to the old Union.

What we now want is a country—a free country—a country not saddened by the footprints of a single slave, and nowhere cursed by the presence of a slaveholder. We want a country which shall not brand the Declaration of Independence as a lie. We want a country whose fundamental institutions we can proudly defend before the highest intelligence and civilization of the age. Hitherto we have opposed European scorn of our slavery with a blush of shame as our best defense. We now want a country in which the obligations of patriotism shall not conflict with fidelity to justice and liberty. We want a country, and are fighting for a country, which shall be free from sectional political parties—free from sectional religious denominations—free from sectional benevolent associations—free from every kind and description of sect, party, and combination of a sectional character. We want a country where men may assemble from any part of it, without prejudice to their interests or peril to their persons.

We are in fact, and from absolute necessity, transplanting the whole South with the higher civilization of the North. The New England schoolhouse is bound to take the place of the Southern whipping post. Not because we love the Negro, but the nation; not because we prefer to do this, because we must or give up the contest and give up the country. We want a country, and are fighting for a country, where social intercourse and commercial relations shall neither be embarrassed nor embittered by the imperious exactions of an insolent slaveholding oligarchy, which required Northern merchants to sell their souls as a condition precedent to selling their goods. We want a country, and are fighting for a country, through the length and breadth of which the literature and learning of any section of it may float to its extremities unimpaired, and thus become the common property of all the people—a country in which no man shall be fined for reading a book, or imprisoned for selling a book—a country where no man may be imprisoned or flogged or sold for learning to read, or teaching a fellow mortal how to read. We want a country, and are fighting for a country, in any part of which to be called an American citizen, shall mean as much as it did to be called a Roman citizen in the palmiest days of the Roman Empire. . . .

—*New York Tribune*, January 14, 1864

54

WE TAKE OUR STAND ON THESE PRINCIPLES

Speaking to the Women's Loyal League at Cooper Institute in New York on February 13, 1864, Douglass condensed his program for racial justice into these four principles.

HERE IS A PART OF THE PLATFORM OF PRINCIPLES UPON WHICH IT SEEMS TO me every loyal man should take his stand at this hour:

FIRST: That this war, which we are compelled to wage against slaveholding rebels and traitors, at untold cost of blood and treasure, shall be, and of right ought to be, an Abolition War.

SECONDLY: That we, the loyal people of the North and of the whole country, while determined to make this a short and final war, will offer no peace, consent to no peace, which shall not be to all intents and purposes an Abolition peace.

THIRDLY: That we regard the whole colored population of the country, in the loyal as well as in the disloyal states, as our countrymen—valuable in peace as laborers, valuable in war as soldiers—entitled to all the rights, protection, and opportunities for achieving distinction enjoyed by any other class of our countrymen.

FOURTHLY: Believing that the white race has nothing to fear from fair competition with the black race, and that the freedom and elevation of one race are not to be purchased or in any manner rightfully subserved by the disfranchisement of another, we shall favor immediate and unconditional emancipation in all the states, invest the black man everywhere with the right to vote and to be voted for, and remove all discriminations against his rights on account of his color, whether as a citizen or as a soldier.

—"Address Delivered in Cooper Institute, New York,"
February 13, 1864

AFTER THE WAR

·⟨━━━━━━━⟩·

As THE EARLY WINTER MONTHS OF 1865 CAME ON, THE CONFEDERACY fell apart. Union armies had control of important sections of the South. Many of its cities lay in ruins. Fields, crops, and homes were destroyed. A third of its white men were dead or wounded. And many—black and white alike—were hungry and homeless.

On March 4, 1865, President Lincoln took again the oath of office, appealing to America "to do all which may achieve a just and lasting peace." On April 9, General Lee surrendered to General Grant at Appomattox Courthouse. The Confederate government evaporated. On April 14, while watching a play at Ford's Theatre in Washington, Lincoln was shot by John Wilkes Booth. He died the next morning without regaining consciousness. His vice president, Andrew Johnson of Tennessee, became president.

Measured by the proportion of casualties to those who fought, the Civil War took the greatest toll of all American wars. Between 33 and 40 percent of the combined Union and Confederate forces were casualties. With the war over, the North turned to a fundamental question: What would be the place of four million freed slaves in the reconstructed Union? Slavery had been not only a system of labor, but the method of racial domination and the foundation of the Southern ruling class. So the future of the former slaves was the pivotal issue for post–Civil War America.

In 1865, Douglass turned forty-seven. Looking back years later on that turning point—the ending of the war and of slavery—he wrote that the abolition of slavery, "the deepest desire and the great labor of my life," had made him feel he had reached the end of "the noblest and best part" of his life. What should he do with the rest of his days?

For a while he thought of quitting public life, retiring to a farm and a peaceful existence. But demands for his oratorical talents poured in, and he

became a well-paid lecturer who could handle many themes, from the anti-slavery movement to how to become a success. Yet none of this took precedence over his burning desire to promote the progress of his people.

He could have gone South, as many urged him, to win election to Congress in the Reconstruction years. Instead, he stayed in the North and continued his role as a national leader in the political struggle of his people. He saw that freedom meant more than simply the end of slavery. True, with freedom came the right to do what you wanted and to go where you wanted to go. But to go from where you had lived and labored, or stay where you were, you had to have work and wages, food and clothing, a roof overhead, and education for yourself and your children.

The free people could not look to the old slaveholders for help. Those whites were bitter and hostile in the disaster of defeat. Didn't the blacks have a right to the land they and their forebears in slavery had cleared and tilled, without ever being paid for their labors? Many ex-slaves argued that they did. The planter class insisted that they did not.

While these questions were being debated, Congress took action. Just as the war was ending, a bill set up the Freedmen's Bureau, putting it under the army's control. The Bureau was to supply food and medicine to both blacks and whites, to try to resettle the freed people in the rural areas of each Southern state, and to regulate the conditions of work.

While many Southern whites wanted the agency to help keep the ex-slaves in line, the blacks demanded that the Bureau work on their behalf. When and where it didn't, they resorted to several methods, including strikes, to force recognition of their rights. Above all, they wanted to free themselves of the efforts by former masters to reestablish control over a cheap labor force. The only way to ensure that was to have land of their own to farm.

Under the new president, Andrew Johnson, governments committed to white supremacy were reestablished by executive order in the states of the former Confederacy. The ex-slaves desiring farms of their own were instead told to sign contracts with their former owners to work for wages. Wages too low to live on and rarely to be paid. The blacks knew that without land of their own, the white planters would keep them in a state of semi-slavery. But the proposal to break up the plantations and parcel them out in sections to the landless farmers, black and white, never became a reality. It was too radical a measure for most, in the government or out, and the hope for a basic change on the land soon faded.

They had lost the war, yes, but the old slaveholders—after a brief era of Reconstruction—would remain the ruling power in the South.

Meanwhile the Congress did pass Constitutional amendments that changed the status of African-Americans. The Thirteenth Amendment (1865) abolished slavery throughout the United States. The Fourteenth Amendment (1868) asserted the equal citizenship of blacks: they were entitled to the "privileges and immunities of citizens," to the "equal protection of the laws," and to protection against being deprived of "life, liberty, and property without due process of law." This amendment did not include the right of black suffrage. That was guaranteed in the Fifteenth Amendment (1870), assuring suffrage for all male citizens, regardless of race or color. (It was the Fourteenth and Fifteenth Amendments that a hundred years later would form the constitutional basis of the civil rights struggle.)

But these were words, promises on paper. Immediately the white South took to terrorism to demonstrate that it meant to restore white supremacy. After repeated acts of violence against African-Americans, Congress adopted the Reconstruction Acts (1867). They put the Union army behind a program of rebuilding the South on the basis of freedom, justice, and equality.

55

THE BALLOT FOR WOMEN

What Douglass had to say, on the platform or through the printed word, had not been carried for some time in a publication of his own. He had shut down Douglass' Monthly *in late 1863, on the mistaken assumption that he would be given an officer's commission to recruit black soldiers in the occupied portions of the South. But when no commission came, he had turned again to the lecture circuit to continue his role as propagandist for the Union cause and for black freedom and equality. For sixteen years his work as editor had been the center of his life and his channel of communication to the world. But other papers welcomed what he had to say, among them the* New York Tribune, *the* Independent, *and the* Anglo-African.

Then in January 1870, the New Era, *sponsored by nine black leaders including Douglass, began publishing weekly in Washington, "in the interests of the colored people of America; not as a separate class, but as a part of the WHOLE PEO-PLE." On September 1 of that year, Douglass bought a half interest in the paper, became its editor, and changed its title to the* New National Era. *His last newspaper, it would run for four years. In one of his early editorials, Douglass took up the issue of the ballot for women.*

. . . WHATEVER MAY BE THOUGHT AS TO THE CONSEQUENCES OF ALLOWING women to vote, it is plain that women themselves are divested of a large measure of their natural dignity by their exclusion from such participation in government. Power is the highest object of human respect. Wisdom, virtue, and all great moral qualities command respect only as powers. Take from money its purchasing power, and it ceases to be the same object of respect. We pity the impotent and respect the powerful everywhere. To deny woman her vote is to abridge her natural and social power and deprive her of a certain measure of respect. Everybody knows that a woman's opinion of any lawmaker would command a larger measure of attention had she the means of making opinion effective at the ballot box. We despise the weak and respect the strong. Such is human nature. Woman herself loses in her own estimation by her enforced exclusion from the elective franchise, just as slaves doubted their own fitness for freedom from the fact of being looked upon as only fit for slaves. While, of course, woman has not fallen so low as the slave in the scale of being (her education and her natural relation to the ruling power rendering such degradation impossible), it is plain that with the ballot in her hand she will ascend a higher elevation in her own thoughts, and even in the thoughts of men, than without that symbol of power. She has power now—mental and moral power—but they are fettered. Nobody is afraid of a chained lion or an empty gun.

It may be said that woman does already exercise political power—that she does through her husband, her father, and others related to her, and hence there is no necessity for extending suffrage to her and allowing her to hold office. . . .

The old slaveholders used to represent the slaves, the rich landowners of other countries represent the poor, and the men in our country claim to represent woman, but the true doctrine of American liberty plainly is that each class and each individual of a class should be allowed to represent himself—that taxation and representation should go together. . . .

Long deprived of the ballot, long branded as an inferior race, long reputed as incapable of exercising the elective franchise, and only recently lifted into the privileges of complete American citizenship, we cannot join with those who would refuse the ballot to women or to any others of mature age and proper residence, who bear the burdens of the government and are obedient to the laws.

—*New National Era,* October 20, 1870

56

STAMP OUT THE KLAN!

The Fifteenth Amendment, designed to protect black suffrage, came to mean less and less with the rise of the Ku Klux Klan in the South. For blacks the right to vote was the heart of Reconstruction. They favored the Republican Party because it was the party that ended slavery and gave them the vote. The other party, the Democrats, had long been the party of the slaveholders. But as African-Americans combined forces with poor whites to adopt progressive state constitutions and pass democratic legislation, the Klan and other secret organizations used every tactic from business pressure to vote-buying to the lash, the torch, and the gun to destroy Reconstruction.

In Georgia alone, for example, during 1868, there were 336 cases of murder or attempted murder of blacks by the Klan. Hundreds of beatings were reported, the victims lashed 300 to 500 times each. For years now the Klan in Mississippi had ridden through the country at night, terrifying, whipping, or murdering whites and blacks who, for one reason or another, were to them undesirable. Most of the Klan leaders were in the upper ranks of white society. Their followers came from every class, from the sons of wealthy planters to illiterate poor whites.

In this editorial Douglass calls for stronger federal efforts to put down the Klan, and for endorsement of President Grant's efforts to do so.

IF EVER THERE WAS A TIME WHEN THE FRIENDS OF REPUBLICAN GOVERNMENT, in accordance with the principles now happily embodied in the organic law of the land, should lay aside all personal considerations and act firmly, unitedly, and with determined energy for the enforcement of the Constitution and the laws in every part of the American Union, that time is now. A rebellion is upon our hands today far more difficult to deal with than that suppressed, but not annihilated, in 1865. Ku-Kluxism, that now moves over the South like the pestilence that walketh in darkness and wasteth at noonday, is only another form of the same old slavery rebellion that hurled against the Union its malignant armies and covered the sea with its pirates a few years ago.

This last form of the rebellion—covert, insidious, secret, striking in the darkness of night, while assuming spotless robes of loyalty in the day—is far more difficult to deal with than an open foe. The South, having failed to gain its ends by a war outside of the Union, has adopted the advice given at the beginning of that war by Henry A. Wise to carry on the war within the Union. It is for us to render this last form as futile as the first—and that is by holding up the hands and seconding the efforts of the same man who, of all men, was most successful in crushing out the rebellion on the open battlefields and behind its strong entrenchments and fortifications. We trusted him then, and not without cause. We have the same reason to trust and support him now. He is for stamping out this murderous Ku-Klux as he stamped out the rebellion. To desert him now, to refuse to sustain him, to seek in any way to weaken his influence, is the surest way to undo the work of the last ten years and remand the Negro to a condition in some respects worse than that from which the war for the Union delivered him. . . .

—*New National Era*, April 6, 1871

57

HATRED FOR PROGRESS

In this article Douglass details some of the "barbaric" means used by the old slaveholding class to resist changes meant to humanize life in the South. He then goes on to illustrate the insanity of their violent efforts to drive out Northerners who had come South to live and work at the close of the Civil War.

THOSE CREDULOUS PEOPLE AT THE NORTH, WHO FONDLY HOPED THAT WITH the overthrow of the rebellion and the triumph of emancipation the barbarism of slavery would begin gradually to give place to civilization, have already discovered their great mistake. So far from the more than five years of peace and freedom having had a humanizing influence upon the old slaveholding population, it has deepened and intensified the barbarism which had so long hung like a black cloud over the slaveholding states. The loss of slavery has deepened their hatred for every kind of progress. The efforts of the government and self-sacrificing Northern men and women to disseminate the blessings of an education among them has met with the most bitter opposition. Schoolhouses are burnt, teachers mobbed and murdered, schools broken up, and every means used to improve the condition of the poorer classes, whether white or black, has only seemed to arouse the wrath of the self-styled ruling classes and to furnish new proof that the barbarism of slavery still exists at the South in all its deformity. Every improvement designed to better the condition of the people, and develop the revenue of the community, is looked upon and treated as a Yankee innovation not to be tolerated for a moment.

But in no way do the old ex-slaveholders of the South exhibit the extent and depth of the barbarism which still holds them in its grasp and influences all their action, as in their evil and wicked opposition to Northern emigration. Even their wholesale murders of loyal men is not so madly stupid as their efforts to prevent Northern men from going among them with their capital and enterprise and their criminal outrages toward those who, trusting to their good faith and common sense, had removed South at the close of the war. They have a motive for these murders, in their political influence. There is undoubtedly a feeling of hatred to Northern men, mixed up with the other motives which expel by threats, mob, or murder Northern men who have removed to the South. But it is mainly the brutalizing, stupefying, and debasing effect upon their natures of the barbarism of slavery. It has not only deadened them to every feeling of decency and humanity and progress, but it has blinded them to their own interests. In expelling Northern emigrants from among them and deterring all others from removing South, they defeat a policy that would enrich them and improve the condition of the whole South without any effort on their part. Such downright brutal stupidity was never before exhibited by any people since the world was created, unless by the Egyptians toward the people of Israel, the Jews by Spain during the reign of Ferdinand and Isabella, or the Jesuits toward the Huguenots. And the result is proving as fatal as in those cases.

We will give a single illustration of the madness of these modern barbarians, which we find in a New York paper, from a gentleman in Corinth, Mississippi. He commences by asserting that the half has not been told in regard to the situation of affairs at the South, and that "a Northern man, no matter what his political opinions are, or how eminent his private character may be, can no more live here in peace and safety than a lamb could among a pack of wolves." He moved to Corinth in 1865. Then all was peace and goodwill. He invested a large amount of money in a manufacturing establishment, which every newspaper is clamoring for, till they seduce capitalists from the North into the net, and then do all they can to embarrass and ruin them. He states that the feeling toward Northern men there "is perfectly fiendish," and that though he has "gone to the very verge of surrendering his Republican principles in his advocacy of the South," any "rowdy could shoot him down in the streets any day with perfect safety from punishment." Not a week passes, he says, without a Ku-Klux murder in the neighborhood of Corinth. He has himself received "two warnings to quit" from the secret Democratic assassins, though he has $25,000 invested there and is adding largely to the wealth of the place. And his conclusion of the whole matter is that the only rule possible there is the one of the bayonet. And he is undoubtedly right.

Such is the besotted madness of the old ex-slaveholding oligarchy of the South. In their blind rage, or rather in the degrading stupidity growing out of the barbarism of slavery, they are utterly incapable of consulting their own interests. How different is the course of all enlightened and civilized communities! Their great study is how to encourage emigration among them. Every inducement possible is held out to them, often in the shape of large tracts of land. Recently a large colony was formed in Chicago with a view of settling in one of the western states or territories. Agents were sent out to select a location. In every state and every territory they met a warm reception, and every possible facility was offered them. Everywhere the colony was assured of a cordial welcome. They finally selected a tract of 55,000 acres in Colorado, upon which the colony settled some weeks ago. They have received from the beginning nothing but kind acts and encouraging words from the whole people and press of the state. They understand that people are the wealth of a state, and, like wise and civilized men, they do what in them lies to secure them. If this colony had attempted to settle in any of the Southern states, they would probably have been met by armed bands of Ku-Klux assassins and half of them murdered and the rest driven back, or, if permitted to reach their destination, assassinated in detail. Such is the difference between barbarism and civilization.

—*New National Era*, April 6, 1871

58

WHAT DOES CHEAP LABOR MEAN?

In 1871, Douglass was elected president of the National Colored Labor Union. It had been organized in 1869, because the National Labor Union, a federation of white trade unions, was excluding blacks from membership and was resisting the hiring of black workers in their shops. They recommended, however, that blacks form separate unions, which could affiliate with the NLU.

Douglass deplored segregated unions while recognizing they were necessary measures of self-defense under the circumstances. In this piece he attacks employers for seeking to import cheap labor from abroad rather than giving work to African-Americans.

HOW VAST AND BOTTOMLESS IS THE ABYSS OF MEANNESS, CRUELTY, AND CRIME sometimes concealed under fair-seeming phrases. . . . Ostensibly the demand for "cheap labor" is made in the interest of improvement and general civilization. It tells of increased wealth and of marvelous transformations of the old and the worthless into the new and valuable. It speaks of increased traveling facilities and larger commercial relations; of long lines of railway graded, and meandering canals constructed; of splendid cities built, and flourishing towns multiplied; of rich mines developed, and useful metals made abundant;

of capacious ships on every sea abroad, and of amply cultivated fields at home; in a word, it speaks of national prosperity, greatness, and happiness.

Alas! However, this is but the outside of the cup and the platter—the beautiful marble without, with its dead men's bones within. Cheap labor is a phrase that has no cheering music for the masses. Those who demand it, and seek to acquire it, have but little sympathy with common humanity. It is the cry of the few against the many. When we inquire who are the men that are continually vociferating for cheap labor, we find not the poor, the simple, and the lowly—not the class who dig and toil for their daily bread; not the landless, feeble, and defenseless portion of society—but the rich and powerful, the crafty and scheming, those who live by the sweat of other men's faces, and who have no intention of cheapening labor by adding themselves to the laboring forces of society. It is the deceitful cry of the fortunate against the unfortunate, of the idle against the industrious, of the taper-figured dandy against the hard-handed working man. Labor is a noble word and expresses a noble idea. Cheap labor, too, seems harmless enough, sounds well to the ear, and looks well upon paper.

But what does it mean? Who does it bless or benefit? The answer is already more than indicated. A moment's thought will show that labor in the mouths of those who seek it, means not cheap labor but the opposite. It means not cheap labor, but dear labor. Not abundant labor, but scarce labor; not more work, but more workmen. It means that condition of things in which the laborers shall be so largely in excess of the work needed to be done that the capitalist shall be able to command all the laborers he wants, at prices only enough to keep the laborer above the point of starvation. It means ease and luxury to the rich, wretchedness and misery to the poor.

The former slave owners of the South want cheap labor—they want it from Germany and from Ireland, they want it from China and Japan, they want it from anywhere in the world but from Africa. They want to be independent of their former slaves and bring their noses to the grindstone. They are not alone in this want, nor is their want a new one. The African slave trade with all its train of horrors was instituted and carried on to supply the opulent landholding inhabitants of this country with cheap labor; and the same lust for gain, the same love of ease and loathing of labor, which originated that infernal traffic, discloses itself in the modern cry for cheap labor and the fair-seeming schemes for supplying the demand. So rapidly does one evil succeed another, and so closely does the succeeding evil resemble the one destroyed, that only a very comprehensive view can afford a basis of faith in the possibility of reform and a recognition of the fact of human progress.

—*New National Era,* August 17, 1871

59

THE RICH GROW RICHER, THE POOR POORER

Hard times hit American workers, black and white, with monotonous regularity. Depression after depression came along to throw millions out of work. All were bitter disasters for working people and their families, no matter how short or long the crisis. And no matter how prosperous some people became—the number of millionaires climbed steadily—the gap between rich and poor widened, for the immense wealth produced by labor was never fairly distributed. In this article Douglass asks which comes first: people or property?

. . . ONE FACT MUST BE APPARENT, THAT IN ALL OLDER COMMUNITIES GOVERNED by the high-pressure principle of competition—the idea which is most tersely expressed in the common saying of "each for himself and the devil take the hindmost"—pauperism is on the increase, penury has become a fixed institution, and the "poverty of the masses the rule, not the exception." The question, whether civilization is designed primarily for man or for property, can have but one direct answer, whatever may be the methods each may think desirable by which to attain that end. The happiness of man must be the primal condition on which any form of society alone can found a title to existence. The civilization, then, looked at in its material aspect alone, which on the one hand constantly increases its wealth-creating capacities and on the other as steadily leaves out of the direct benefits thereof at least seven-tenths of all who live within its influence, cannot have realized the fundamental condition of its continuance.

That society is a failure in which the large majority of its members, without any direct fault of their own, would, if any accidental circumstances deprived them for a month of the opportunity of earning regular wages, be dependent upon private or public charity for daily bread. Yet such is the actual condition of even favored American labor. It is an appreciation of this dependence that gives such formidable impulse to the discontent of labor. It is the general ignorance of equitable remedies which makes that discontent so dangerous. The movement is fundamental. It grows with great rapidity. It will compel a hearing by the very force of numbers if nothing else. . . .

No movement which involves vast numbers as this does can be safely denounced or ignored. It must be met, treated fairly, and examined into, or the whole fabric will be wrenched by violent convulsions. There is always justice in the general demand. Ignorance may warp, prejudice contract, but the guiding impulse is one that seeks to right some wrong.

Inquiry into the condition of labor is the first step. Let the good people know how much truth there is in the reiterated charges that are made "that the rich grow richer, the poor poorer"; that in all our manufacturing and industrial centers the gulf between classes is steadily widening, and that all the conditions under which the United States has hitherto been the paradise of labor are rapidly changing and steadily deviating; that, in fact, we are taking on the degrading conditions of European society. Somewhat of this is true. Enough, we believe, to warrant full examination into its causes and investigation into the remedies, if there be any.

—*New National Era*, October 12, 1871

60

WHY WE WANT MIXED SCHOOLS

Douglass called for equal treatment in the church, on the streetcar, in the hotel, in the school. He believed that an integrated public school education would diminish racism and bring people of all races closer together. As with labor unions, he accepted separate black schools only as a temporary measure until schools could be open to all. To him education was always central to ideas about social reform. "It means light and liberty," he said. "To deny education to any people is one of the greatest crimes against human nature."

In this editorial he spells out why he believes mixed schools in the South would benefit everyone.

THE QUESTION OF THE ESTABLISHMENT OF COMMON SCHOOLS IN THE DISTRICT of Columbia in which caste prejudices will not be nurtured, is now agitating the people of this community. . . .

Throughout the South all the schools should be mixed. From our observations during a trip to the South, we are convinced that the interests of the poor whites and the colored people are identical. Both are ignorant, and both are the tools of designing educated white men; and the poor whites are more particularly used to further schemes opposed to their own best interests. In that section everything that will bring the poor white man and the colored man closer together should be done; they should be taught to make common cause against the rich landholders of the South who never regarded a poor white man of as much importance as they did slaves. Educate the poor white children and the colored children together; let them grow up to know that color makes no difference as to the rights of a man; that both the black man and the white man are at home; that the country is as much the country of one as of the other; and that both together must make it a valuable country.

Now in the South the poor white man is taught that he is better than the black man, and not as good as the 250,000 slaveholders of former days; the result is that the slaveholders command the poor white man to murder the black man, to burn down his schoolhouses, and to in every conceivable manner maltreat him—and the command is obeyed. This tends to make the ex-slaveholder more powerful and is of no good to the poor white who is really as much despised as the Negro. The cunning ex-slaveholder sets those who should be his enemies to fighting each other and thus diverts attention from himself. Educate the colored children and white children together in your day and night schools throughout the South, and they will learn to know each other better and be better able to cooperate for mutual benefit.

We want mixed schools not because our colored schools are inferior to white schools, not because colored instructors are inferior to white instructors, but because we want to do away with a system that exalts one class and debases another. . . .

Our idea of mixed schools comprehends the employment of colored as well as white teachers, and of neither unless they are competent. Anything less than this would be fostering the very caste distinctions of which we all complain. It is saying to the colored child you may learn and acquire an abundance of intelligence, but you must never hope to know enough to be able to teach a primary school composed of white children and colored children. . . .

We look to mixed schools to teach that worth and ability are to be the criterion of manhood and not race and color.

—*New National Era*, May 2, 1872

61

IN MEMORY OF ABRAHAM LINCOLN

One of the most famous speeches of Douglass's career was given in April 1876, at the dedication in Washington of the Freedmen's Memorial Monument to Lincoln. Despite all his reservations about Lincoln and his strong criticism of him during the war years, Douglass saw Lincoln as a great man, to be ranked with those two other heroes of Douglass—John Brown and Toussaint L'Ouverture. A champion of black liberation in his own distinctive way, Lincoln, like the others, fell a martyr to the struggle for human dignity. In these passages from the oration, Douglass describes Lincoln's achievements and takes the measure of the man so well fitted to carry out his mission.

. . . THOUGH THE UNION WAS MORE TO HIM THAN OUR FREEDOM OR OUR future, under his wise and beneficent rule we saw ourselves gradually lifted from the depths of slavery to the heights of liberty and manhood; under his wise and beneficent rule, and by measures approved and vigorously pressed by him, we saw that the handwriting of ages, in the form of prejudice and proscription, was rapidly fading away from the face of our whole country; under his rule, and in due time, about as soon after all as the country could tolerate the strange spectacle, we saw our brave sons and brothers laying off the rags of bondage and being clothed all over in the blue uniforms of the

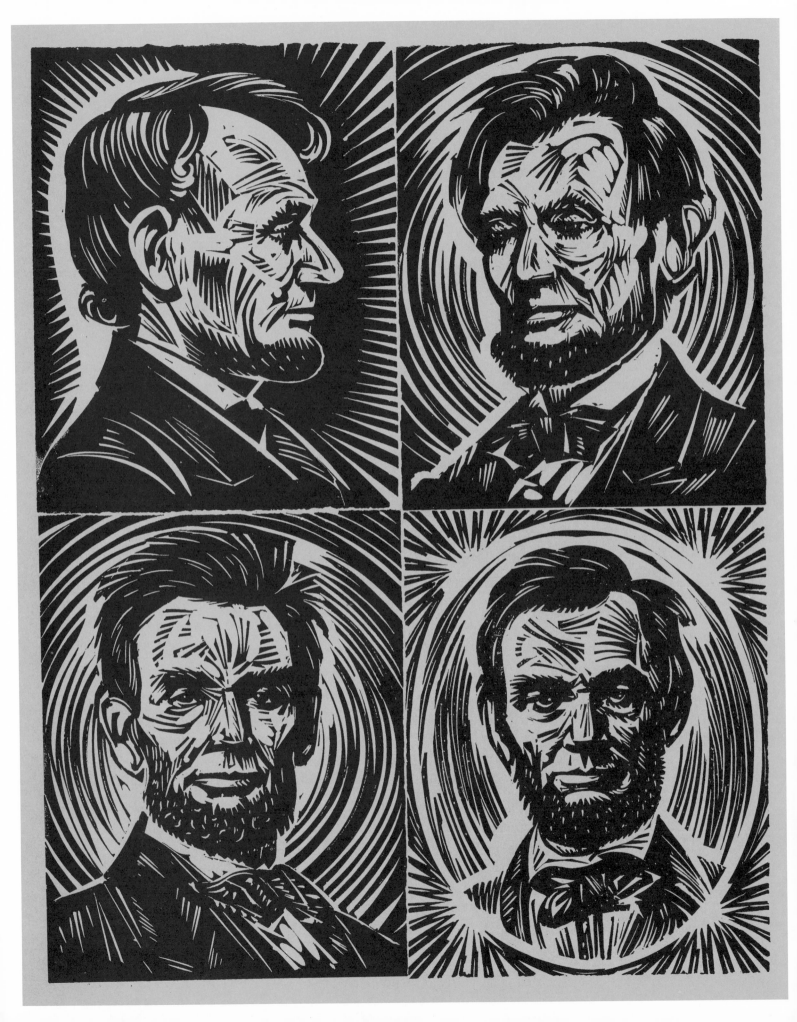

soldiers of the United States; under his rule we saw two hundred thousand of our dark and dusky people responding to the call of Abraham Lincoln and, with muskets on their shoulders and eagles on their buttons, timing their high footsteps to liberty and union under the national flag; under his rule we saw the independence of the black republic of Haiti, the special object of slave-holding aversion and horror, fully recognized, and her minister, a colored gentleman, duly received here in the city of Washington; under his rule we saw the internal slave trade, which so long disgraced the nation, abolished, and slavery abolished in the District of Columbia; under his rule we saw for the first time the law enforced against the foreign slave trade, and the first slave trader hanged like any other pirate or murderer; under his rule, assisted by the greatest captain of our age, and his inspiration, we saw the Confederate States, based upon the idea that our race must be slaves, and slaves forever, battered to pieces and scattered to the four winds; under his rule, and in the fullness of time, we saw Abraham Lincoln, after giving the slaveholders three months' grace in which to save their hateful slave system, penning the immortal paper, which, though special in its language, was general in its principles and effect, making slavery forever impossible in the United States. Though we waited long, we saw all this and more.

Can any colored man, or any white man friendly to the freedom of all men, ever forget the night which followed the first day of January 1863, when the world was to see if Abraham Lincoln would prove to be as good as his word? I shall never forget that memorable night, when in a distant city I waited and watched at a public meeting with three thousand others not less anxious than myself, for the word of deliverance which we have heard read today. Nor shall I ever forget the outburst of joy and thanksgiving that rent the air when the lightning brought to us the Emancipation Proclamation. In that happy hour we forgot all delay, and forgot all tardiness, forgot that the president had bribed the rebels to lay down their arms by a promise to withhold the bolt which would smite the slave system with destruction; and we were thenceforward willing to allow the president all the latitude of time, phraseology, and every honorable device that statesmanship might require for the achievement of a great and beneficient measure of liberty and progress. . . .

His great mission was to accomplish two things: first, to save his country from dismemberment and ruin; and, second, to free his country from the great crime of slavery. To do one or the other, or both, he must have the earnest sympathy and the powerful cooperation of his loyal fellow countrymen. Without this primary and essential condition to success, his efforts must have been vain and utterly fruitless. Had he put the abolition of slavery before the salvation of the Union, he would have inevitably driven from him a powerful class of the American people and rendered resistance to rebellion impossible. Viewed from the genuine abolition ground, Mr. Lincoln seemed tardy, cold, dull, and indifferent; but measuring him by the sentiment he was bound as a statesman to consult, he was swift, zealous, radical, and determined. . . .

The judgment of the present hour is, that taking him for all in all, measuring the tremendous magnitude of the work before him, considering the necessary means to ends, and surveying the end from the beginning, infinite wisdom has seldom sent any man into the world better fitted for his mission than Abraham Lincoln. His birth, his training, and his natural endowments, both mental and physical, were strongly in his favor. Born and reared among the lowly, a stranger to wealth and luxury, compelled to grapple single-handed with the flintiest hardships of life, from tender youth to sturdy manhood, he grew strong in the manly and heroic qualities demanded by the great mission to which he was called by the votes of his countrymen. The hard condition of his early life, which would have depressed and broken down weaker men, only gave greater life, vigor, and buoyancy to the heroic spirit of Abraham Lincoln. . . .

Had Abraham Lincoln died from any of the numerous ills to which flesh is heir; had he reached that good old age of which his vigorous constitution and his temperate habits gave promise; had he been permitted to see the end of his great work; had the solemn curtain of death come down but gradually—we should still have been smitten with a heavy grief and treasured his name lovingly. But dying as he did die, by the red hand of violence, killed, assassinated, taken off without warning, not because of personal hate—for no men who knew Abraham Lincoln could hate him—but because of his fidelity to union and liberty, he is doubly dear to us, and his memory will be precious forever. . . .

—"Inaugural Ceremonies of the Freedmen's Memorial Monument to Abraham Lincoln," Washington City, April 14, 1876

62

THE COLOR LINE

During the postwar years, Douglass received several appointments to office by Republican presidents. None of these positions carried political weight, which must have been disappointing to a man of Douglass's stature who had a right to expect more. Some of Douglass's friends saw these appointments as screens to conceal the ending of any effort by the federal government to do something significant for African-Americans. As the Republicans increasingly became the party of wealth and big business, their humanitarian concerns died. Nevertheless, Douglass maintained his loyalty to the party that had ended slavery.

With the entry of Rutherford B. Hayes to the White House, Radical Reconstruction came to a close. As part of a bargain over power between the two major parties, called the Compromise of 1877, upon taking office, Hayes withdrew the last federal troops from the South. The whites who had once imposed slavery were again free to do as they liked with the black population. The "home rule" restored to the South by Hayes would last another eighty years. Not until the Little Rock school crisis of 1957 would federal troops be used to uphold the Constitution and the law in the South.

Hayes said he had faith in "the great mass of intelligent white men" to protect the blacks' rights. It was a faith worth very little. In June 1881, Douglass wrote a scorching article for the North American Review *on the stubborn persistence of racism in every part of American society.*

FEW EVILS ARE LESS ACCESSIBLE TO THE FORCE OF REASON, OR MORE TENACIOUS of life and power, than a long-standing prejudice. It is a moral disorder, which creates the conditions necessary to its own existence and fortifies itself by refusing all contradiction. It paints a hateful picture according to its own diseased imagination and distorts the features of the fancied original to suit the portrait. As those who believe in the visibility of ghosts can easily see them, so it is always easy to see repulsive qualities in those we despise and hate.

Prejudice of race has at some time in their history afflicted all nations. . . . Of all the races and varieties of men which have suffered from this feeling, the colored people of this country have endured most. They can resort to no disguises which will enable them to escape its deadly aim. They carry in front the evidence which marks them for persecution. They stand at the extreme point of difference from the Caucasian race, and their African origin can be instantly recognized, though they may be several removes from the typical African race. They may remonstrate like Shylock—"Hath not a Jew eyes? Hath not a Jew hands, organs, dimensions, senses, affections, passions? Fed with the same food, hurt with the same weapons, subject to the same diseases, healed by the same means, warmed and cooled by the same summer and winter, as a Christian is?"—but such eloquence is unavailing. They are Negroes—and that is enough, in the eye of this unreasoning prejudice, to justify indignity and violence.

In nearly every department of American life they are confronted by this insidious influence. It fills the air. It meets them at the workshop and factory when they apply for work. It meets them at the church, at the hotel, at the ballot box, and worst of all, it meets them in the jury box. Without crime or offense against law or gospel, the colored man is the Jean Valjean of American society. He has escaped from the galleys, and hence all presumptions are against him. The workshop denies him work, and the inn denies him shelter; the ballot box a fair vote, and the jury box a fair trial. He has ceased to be the slave of an individual, but has in some sense become the slave of society. He may not now be bought and sold like a beast in the market, but he is the trammeled victim of a prejudice well calculated to repress his manly ambition, paralyze his energies, and make him a dejected and spiritless man, if not a sullen enemy of society, fit to prey upon life and property and to make trouble generally.

When this evil spirit is judge, jury, and prosecutor, nothing less than overwhelming evidence is sufficient to overcome the force of unfavorable presumptions.

Everything against the person with the hated color is promptly taken for granted; while everything in his favor is received with suspicion and doubt. . . .

If what is called the instinctive aversion of the white race for the colored, when analyzed, is seen to be the same as that which men feel or have felt toward other objects wholly apart from color; if it should be the same as that sometimes exhibited by the haughty and rich to the humble and poor, the same as the Brahmin feels toward the lower caste, the same as the Norman felt toward the Saxon, the same as that cherished by the Turk against Christians, the same as Christians have felt toward the Jews, the same as that which murders a Christian in Wallachia, calls him a "dog" in Constantinople, oppresses and persecutes a Jew in Berlin, hunts down a socialist in St. Petersburg, drives a Hebrew from an hotel at Saratoga, that scorns the Irishman in London, the same as Catholics once felt for Protestants, the same as that which insults, abuses, and kills the Chinaman on the Pacific slope—then may we well enough affirm that this prejudice really has nothing whatever to do with race or color, and that it has its motive and mainspring in some other source with which the mere facts of color and race have nothing to do. . . .

Slavery, ignorance, stupidity, servility, poverty, dependence are undesirable conditions. When these shall cease to be coupled with color, there will be no color line drawn.

It may help in this direction to observe a few of the inconsistencies of the color-line feeling, for it is neither uniform in its operations nor consistent in its principles. . . . Statesmen of the South will tell you that the Negro is too ignorant and stupid to properly exercise the elective franchise, and yet his greatest offense is that he acts with the only party intelligent enough in the eyes of the nation to legislate for the country. In one breath they tell us that the Negro is so weak in intellect and so destitute of manhood that he is but the echo of designing white men, and yet in another they will virtually tell you that the Negro is so clear in his moral perceptions, so firm in purpose, so steadfast in his convictions, that he cannot be persuaded by arguments or intimidated by threats, and that nothing but the shotgun can restrain him from voting for the men and measures he approves.

They shrink back in horror from contact with the Negro as a man and a gentleman, but like him very well as a barber, waiter, coachman, or cook. . . . Formerly it was said he was incapable of learning, and at the same time it was a crime against the State for any man to teach him to read. Today he is said to be originally and permanently inferior to the white race, and yet wild apprehensions are expressed lest six millions of this inferior race will somehow or other manage to rule over thirty-five millions of the superior race. If inconsistency can prove the hollowness of anything, certainly the emptiness of this pretense that color has any terrors is easily shown. . . .

—*North American Review*, June 1881

63

Assimilation Is Life; Separation Is Death

In 1883, Douglass examined what the triumphant return of the old master class to power meant for his people. After going over the grim facts he attempted to impart some sense of hope that life would get better, that justice was not a dead issue, that the whole American people would one day live together in peace. He clung to his belief that white Americans would gradually see the harm racism did, to themselves and to everyone else. And he ended with a strong commitment to assimilation—not isolation—as "our true policy and our natural destiny. Unification for us is life; separation is death." He offered these ideas to a Washington audience marking the twenty-first anniversary of emancipation in the District of Columbia.

. . . As the war for the Union recedes into the misty shadows of the past and the Negro is no longer needed to assault forts and stop rebel bullets, he is, in some sense, of less importance. Peace with the old master class has been war to the Negro. As the one has risen, the other has fallen. The reaction has been sudden, marked, and violent. It has swept the Negro from all the legislative halls of the Southern states and from those of the Congress of the United States. It has, in many cases, driven him from the ballot box and the jury box. The situation has much in it for serious thought, but nothing to cause despair. . . .

Time and events which have done so much for us in the past, will, I trust, not do less for us in the future. The moral government of the universe is on our side and cooperates, with all honest efforts, to lift up the downtrodden and oppressed in all lands, whether the oppressed be white or black. . . .

It is his sad lot to live in a land where all presumptions are arrayed against him, unless we except the presumption of inferiority and worthlessness. If his course is downward, he meets very little resistance, but if upward, his way is disputed at every turn of the road. If he comes in rags and in wretchedness, he answers the public demand for a Negro and provokes no anger, though he may provoke derision; but if he presumes to be a gentleman and a scholar, he is then entirely out of his place. He excites resentment and calls forth stern and bitter opposition. If he offers himself to a builder as a mechanic, to a client as a lawyer, to a patient as a physician, to a university as a professor, or to a department as a clerk, no matter what may be his ability or his attainments, there is a presumption based upon his color or his previous condition, of incompetency, and if he succeeds at all, he has to do so against this most discouraging presumption.

It is a real calamity in this country for any man, guilty or not guilty, to be accused of crime, but it is an incomparably greater calamity for any colored man to be so accused. Justice is often painted with bandaged eyes. She is described in forensic eloquence as utterly blind to wealth or poverty, high or low, white or black, but a mask of iron, however thick, could never blind American justice when a black man happens to be on trial. Here, even more than elsewhere, he will find all presumptions of law and evidence against him. It is not so much the business of his enemies to prove him guilty, as it is the business of himself to prove his innocence. The reasonable doubt, which is usually interposed to have the life and liberty of a white man charged with crime, seldom has any force or effect when a colored man is accused of crime. . . .

A still greater misfortune to the Negro is that the press, that engine of omnipotent power, usually tries him in advance of the courts, and when once his case is decided in the newspapers, it is easy for the jury to bring in its verdict of "guilty as indicted."

In many parts of our common country, the action of courts and juries is entirely too slow for the impetuosity of the people's justice. When the black man is accused, the mob takes the law into its own hands and whips, shoots, stabs, hangs, or burns the accused, simply upon the allegation or suspicion of crime. . . .

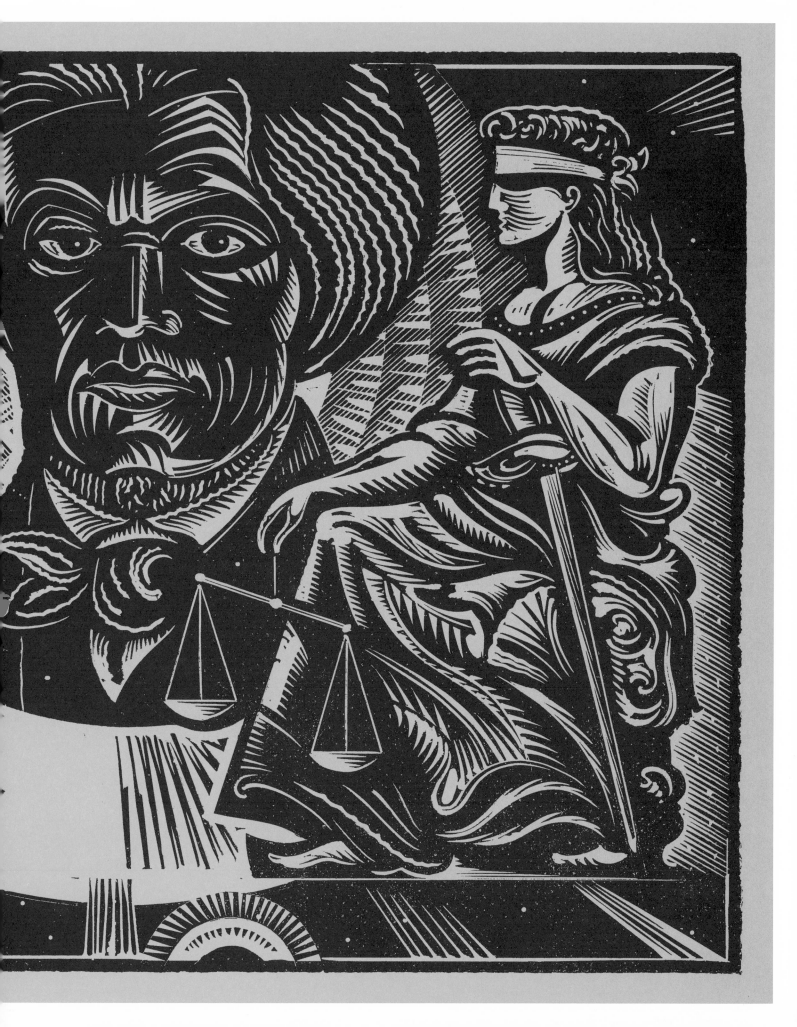

Another feature of the situation is that this mob violence is seldom rebuked by the press and the pulpit in its immediate neighborhood. Because the public opinion, which sustains and makes possible such outrages, intimidates both press and pulpit.

Besides, nobody expects that those who participate in such mob violence will ever be held answerable to the law and punished. Of course, judges are not always unjust, nor juries always partial in cases of this class, but I affirm that I have here given you no picture of the fancy, and I have alleged no point incapable of proof, and drawn no line darker or denser than the terrible reality. The situation, my colored fellow citizens, is discouraging, but with all its hardships and horrors, I am neither desperate nor despairing as to the future.

One ground of hope is found in the fact referred to in the beginning, and that is, the discussion concerning the Negro still goes on.

The country in which we live is happily governed by ideas as well as by laws, and no black man need despair while there is an audible and earnest assertion of justice and right on his behalf. He may be riddled with bullets, or roasted over a slow fire by the mob, but his cause cannot be shot or burned or otherwise destroyed. Like the impalpable ghost of the murdered Hamlet, it is immortal. All talk of its being a dead issue is a mistake. It may for a time be buried, but it is not dead. Tariffs, free trade, civil service, and river and harbor bills may for a time cover it, but it will rise again, and again, and again, with increased life and vigor. Every year adds to the black man's numbers. Every year adds to his wealth and to his intelligence. These will speak for him.

There is a power in numbers, wealth, and intelligence which can never be despised nor defied. All efforts thus far to diminish the Negro's importance as a man and as a member of the American body politic have failed. . . .

Without putting my head to the ground, I can even now hear the anxious inquiry as to when this discussion of the Negro will cease. When will he cease to be a bone of contention between the two great parties? Speaking for myself, I can honestly say I wish it to cease. . . . The demand for Negro rights would have ceased long since but for the existence of a sufficient and substantial cause for its continuance. . . .

What Abraham Lincoln said in respect of the United States is as true of the colored people as of the relations of those states. They cannot remain half slave and half free. You must give them all or take from them all. Until this half-and-half condition is ended, there will be just ground of complaint. You will have an aggrieved class, and this discussion will go on. Until the colored man's right to practice at the bar of our courts and sit upon juries shall be the universal law and practice of the land, this discussion will go on. Until the courts of the country shall grant the colored man a fair trial and a just verdict, this discussion will go on. Until color shall cease to be a bar to equal participation in the offices and honors of the country, this discussion will go on. Until the trade unions and the workshops of the country shall cease to proscribe the colored man and prevent his children from learning useful trades, this discussion will go on. Until the American people shall make character, and not color, the criterion of respectability, this discussion will go on. Until men like Bishops Payne and Campbell shall cease to be driven from respectable railroad cars at the South, this discussion will go on. In a word, until truth and humanity shall cease to be living ideas, and mankind shall sink back into moral darkness, and the world shall put evil for good, bitter for sweet, and darkness for light, this discussion will go on. Until all humane ideas and civilization shall be banished from the world, this discussion will go on. . . .

What is to be the future of the colored people of this country? Some change in their condition seems to be looked for by thoughtful men everywhere; but what that change will be, no one yet has been able with certainty to predict. . . .

In every great movement men are prepared by preceding events for those which are to come. We neither know the evil nor the good which may be in store for us. Twenty-five years ago the system of slavery seemed impregnable. Cotton was king, and the civilized world acknowledged his sway. Twenty-five years ago no man could have foreseen that in less than ten years from that time no master would wield a lash and no slave would clank a chain in the United States.

Who at that time dreamed that Negroes would ever be seen as we have seen them today, marching through the streets of this superb city, the capital of this great nation, with eagles on their buttons, muskets on their shoulders, and swords by their sides, timing their high footsteps to the "Star-Spangled Banner" and the "Red, White, and Blue"? Who at that time dreamed that colored men would ever sit in the House of Representatives and in the Senate of the United States?

With a knowledge of the events of the last score of years, with a knowledge of the sudden and startling changes which have already come to pass, I am not prepared to say what the future will be. . . .

There is but one destiny, it seems to me, left for us, and that is to make ourselves and be made by others a part of the American people in every sense of the word. Assimilation and not isolation is our true policy and our natural destiny. Unification for us is life: separation is death. We cannot afford to set up for ourselves a separate political party or adopt for ourselves a political creed apart from the rest of our fellow citizens. Our own interests will be subserved by a generous care for the interests of the nation at large. All the political, social, and literary forces around us tend to unification.

I am the more inclined to accept this solution because I have seen the steps already taken in that direction. The American people have their prejudices, but they have other qualities as well. They easily adapt themselves to inevitable conditions, and all their tendency is to progress, enlightenment, and to the universal.

—"Address of Hon. Frederick Douglass, delivered in the
Congregational Church, Washington, D.C., April 16, 1883, on the
Twenty-First Anniversary of Emancipation in the District of Columbia"

64

The Destruction of Civil Rights

For years during the 1870s, some radical Republicans had tried to get a civil rights bill through Congress, but without success. Finally, a watered-down version of their proposals was adopted as the Civil Rights Act of 1875. Little attention was paid, however, to its provisions for the protection of the rights of African-Americans. With the ending of Reconstruction, the Supreme Court, made up of nine Repub-

licans, supported the growing national opinion that blacks were not entitled to the same rights as whites.

In 1883, the Court, by a vote of 8 to 1, issued a decision on civil rights. (The lone dissenter was Justice John Marshall Harlan.) Only the state legislatures, said the Court, and not the United States Congress had jurisdiction over a citizen's rights. It nullified the Civil Rights Law of 1875, and sanctioned the segregation of African-Americans by individuals in all the states. The Court had opened the door for the passage of Jim Crow laws throughout the South. Not until eighty-one years later, with the passage of the Civil Rights Act of 1964, would the Court's decision be overturned.

In this speech in Washington, Douglass voiced the outrage felt by his people.

. . . The Supreme Court of the United States, in the exercise of its high and vast constitutional power, has suddenly and unexpectedly decided that the law intended to secure to colored people the civil rights guaranteed to them by the following provision of the Constitution of the United States is unconstitutional and void. Here it is:

"No State," says the Fourteenth Amendment, "shall make or enforce any law which shall abridge the privileges or immunities of citizens of the United States; nor shall any State deprive any person of life, liberty, or property without due process of law; nor deny any person within its jurisdiction the equal protection of the laws."

Now, when a bill has been discussed for weeks and months, and even years, in the press and on the platform, in Congress and out of Congress; when it has been calmly debated by the clearest heads, and the most skillful and learned lawyers in the land; when every argument against it has been over and over again carefully considered and fairly answered; when its constitutionality has been especially discussed, pro and con; when it has passed the United States House of Representatives and has been solemnly enacted by the United States Senate, perhaps the most imposing legislative body in the world; when such a bill has been submitted to the cabinet of the nation, composed of the ablest men in the land; when it has passed under the scrutinizing eye of the attorney general of the United States; when the executive of the nation has given to it his name and formal approval; when it has taken its place upon the statute book and has remained there for nearly a decade, and the country has largely assented to it, you will agree with me that the reasons for declaring such a law unconstitutional and void should be strong, irresistible, and absolutely conclusive.

Inasmuch as the law in question is a law in favor of liberty and justice, it ought to have had the benefit of any doubt which could arise as to its strict constitutionality. This, I believe, will be the view taken of it, not only by laymen like myself, but by eminent lawyers as well. . . .

This decision has inflicted a heavy calamity upon seven millions of the people of this country and left them naked and defenseless against the actions of a malignant, vulgar, and pitiless prejudice. It presents the United States before the world as a nation utterly destitute of power to protect the rights of its own citizens upon its own soil.

It can claim service and allegiance, loyalty and life, of them, but it cannot protect them against the most palpable violation of the rights of human nature, rights to secure which governments are established. It can tax their bread and tax their blood, but has no protecting power for their persons. Its national power extends only to the District of Columbia and the Territories—where the people have no votes and where the land has no people. All else is subject to the states. In the name of common sense, I ask, what right have we to call ourselves a nation, in view of this decision and this utter destitution of power?

This decision of the Supreme Court admits that the Fourteenth Amendment is a prohibition on the states. It admits that a state shall not abridge the privileges or immunities of citizens of the United States, but commits the seeming absurdity of allowing the people of a state to do what it prohibits the state itself from doing.

It used to be thought that the whole was more than a part; that the greater included the less, and that what was unconstitutional for a state to do was equally unconstitutional for an individual member of a state to do. What is a state, in the absence of the people who compose it? Land, air, and water. That is all. As individuals, the people of the State of South Carolina may stamp out the rights of the Negro wherever they please, so long as they do not do so as a state. All the parts can violate the Constitution, but the whole cannot. It is not the act itself, according to this decision, that is unconstitutional. The unconstitutionality of the cause depends wholly upon the party committing the act. If the state commits it, it is wrong; if the citizen of the state commits it, it is right.

O consistency, thou art indeed a jewel! What does it matter to a colored citizen that a state may not insult and outrage him, if a citizen of a state may? The effect upon him is the same, and it was just this effect that the framers of the Fourteenth Amendment plainly intended by that article to prevent.

It was the act, not the instrument, which was prohibited. It meant to protect the newly enfranchised citizen from injustice and wrong, not merely from a state, but from the individual members of a state. It meant to give him the protection to which his citizenship, his loyalty, his allegiance, and his services entitled him, and this meaning, and this purpose, and this intention is now declared unconstitutional and void by the Supreme Court of the United States.

I say again, fellow citizens, O for a Supreme Court which shall be as true, as vigilant, as active, and exacting in maintaining laws enacted for the protection of human rights as in other days was that Court for the destruction of human rights! . . .

—"Proceedings of the Civil Rights Mass Meeting held at Lincoln Hall, October 22, 1883"

65

I HAVE NO APOLOGY

In August 1882, Anna Murray Douglass, Frederick Douglass's wife, died, and on January 24, 1884, he married Helen Pitts. He was now sixty-six, and she was forty-five. Her parents were abolitionists from upstate New York, where they had known Douglass, and like them, their daughter, a graduate of Mt. Holyoke Seminary, espoused women's rights. At the news of the interracial marriage, "false friends of both colors," wrote Douglass bitterly, had "loaded him with reproach." His second marriage was consistent with his firm view that black and white Americans must eventually amalgamate. He envisioned an America where race and color were no longer an issue. He refused to be confined in his personal life by attitudes and values shaped by the long history of racism. He held all forms of racial exclusiveness or constraint to be wrong and harmful.

In a letter to his old friend Elizabeth Cady Stanton, Douglass said that his second marriage was a purely personal matter.

WASHINGTON, D.C.
MAY 30, 1884

MY DEAR MRS. STANTON:

I am very glad to find, as I do find by your kind good letter, that I have made no mistake in respect of your feeling concerning my marriage. I have known you and your love of liberty so long and well that, without one word from you on the subject, I had recorded your word and vote against the clamor raised against my marriage to a white woman. To those who find fault with me on this account, I have no apology to make. My wife and I have simply obeyed the convictions of our own minds and hearts in a matter wherein we alone were concerned and about which nobody has any right to interfere. I could never have been at peace with my own soul or held up my head among men had I allowed the fear of popular clamor to deter me from following my convictions as to this marriage. I should have gone to my grave a self-accused and a self-convicted moral coward. Much as I respect the good opinion of my fellow men, I do not wish it at expense of my own self-respect.

Circumstances have, during the last forty years, thrown me much more into white society than in that of colored people. While true to the rights of the colored race, my nearest personal friends, owing to association and common sympathy and aims, have been white people, and as men choose wives from friends and associates, it is not strange that I have so chosen my wife and that she has chosen me. You, Dear Mrs. Stanton, could have found a straight, smooth, and pleasant road through the world had you allowed the world to decide for you your sphere in life, that is, had you allowed it to sink your moral and intellectual individuality into nonentity. But you have nobly asserted your own and the rights of your sex, and the world will know hereafter that you have lived and worked beneficently in the world.

You have made both Mrs. Douglass and myself very glad and happy by your letter, and we both give you our warmest thanks for it. Helen is a braver woman that I am a man and bears the assaults of popular prejudice more serenely than I do. No sigh or complaint escapes her. She is steady, firm, and strong and meets the gaze of the world with a tranquil heart and unruffled brow. I am amazed by her heroic bearing, and I am greatly strengthened by it. She has sometimes said she would not regret though the storm of opposition were ten times greater. . . .

—Elizabeth Cady Stanton Manuscripts, Library of Congress

66

THIS BURNING SHAME

In his closing years, Douglass witnessed the violence against his people reach a hideous climax. During the decade from 1890 to 1900, there would be recorded 1,127 mob murders by hanging, burning, shooting, or beating, almost all in the South. African-Americans were being treated worse now than at any other time since the Civil War ended. Douglass said in 1892 that the South alone was not responsible for "this burning shame . . . The sin against the Negro is both sectional and national; and until the voice of the North shall be heard in emphatic condemnation and withering reproach against these continued ruthless mob-law murders, it will remain equally involved with the South in this common crime."

That year Douglass met Ida B. Wells, a brilliant thirty-year-old who was the daughter of slaves. She was exposing lynching in fiery articles in the black press or by pamphlets, giving names, dates, and places with detailed descriptions of the cruelty of the mobs. Lynching, the young journalist contended, was a form of intimidation to preserve the plantation economy and the white ballot box in the South. Douglass joined with Wells and others in campaigning for a strong commitment by the Republicans to federal action to protect the lives and civil rights of African-Americans in the South. But his party would give no assurance of a federal program to stop lynching.

In 1894, Douglass gave a major speech, "Why Is the Negro Lynched?" He took up the epidemic of mob law, the attitude of the upper class toward it, the excuses given for lynching, the general lack of respect in the South for human life, the appalling economic conditions imposed upon blacks, and then demolished the common assumption that there was a "Negro problem."

"What the real problem is we all ought to know," he said. "It is not a Negro problem, but in every sense a great national problem. It involves the question,

whether after all our boasted civilization, our Declaration of Independence, our matchless Constitution, our sublime Christianity, our wise statesmanship, we as a people possess virtue enough to solve this problem in accordance with wisdom and justice, and to the advantage of both races."

He concluded with this passage on how to solve the problem.

BUT HOW CAN THIS PROBLEM BE SOLVED? I WILL TELL YOU HOW IT CANNOT be solved. It cannot be solved by keeping the Negro poor, degraded, ignorant, and half-starved, as I have shown is now being done in Southern states.

It cannot be solved by keeping back the wages of the laborer by fraud, as is now being done by the landlords of the South. It cannot be done by ballot-box stuffing, by falsifying election returns, or by confusing the Negro voter by cunning devices. It cannot be done by repealing all federal laws enacted to secure honest elections. It can, however, be done, and very easily done, for where there is a will there is a way.

Let the white people of the North and South conquer their prejudice.

Let the Northern press and pulpit proclaim the gospel of truth and justice against the war now being made upon the Negro.

Let the American people cultivate kindness and humanity.

Let the South abandon the system of mortgage labor and cease to make the Negro a pauper by paying him dishonest scrip for his honest labor.

Let them give up the idea that they can be free while making the Negro a slave. Let them give up the idea that to degrade the colored man is to elevate the white man. Let them cease putting new wine into old bottles and mending old garments with new cloth.

They are not required to do much. They are only required to undo the evil they have done in order to solve this problem.

In old times when it was asked, "How can we abolish slavery?" the answer was "Quit stealing."

The same is the solution of the race problem today. The whole thing can be done simply by no longer violating the amendment of the Constitution of the United States, and no longer evading the claims of justice. If this were done, there would be no Negro problem or national problem to vex the South or to vex the nation.

Let the organic law of the land be honestly sustained and obeyed. Let the political parties cease to palter in a double sense, and live up to the noble declarations we find in their platforms. Let the statesmen of our country live up to their convictions. In the language of ex-Senator Ingalls: "Let the nation try justice and the problem will be solved."

—*Frederick Douglass, The Lesson of the Hour,* pamphlet, 1894

AFTERWORD

IN THE LAST TWO DECADES OF HIS LIFE, DOUGLASS, ALWAYS THE STEADFAST Republican, received several offices from the leaders of his party. President Rutherford B. Hayes appointed him marshal of the District of Columbia (1877–1880). It was the first time the Senate approved the appointment of an African-American. Perhaps the Southerners could easily make such a concession in view of the much greater concessions the president had made to white supremacists in withdrawing federal troops from their states.

A few years later President James Garfield gave the job of marshal to a personal friend and shifted Douglass to the post of the District's Recorder of Deeds (1881–1886). In 1889, when Douglass was seventy-one, President Benjamin Harrison appointed him minister to Haiti, where he served until mid-1891.

In the few years left to him, Douglass witnessed how badly the condition of his people was deteriorating. He looked to the new generation, represented by Ida B. Wells, to join him in fighting the battle against racism and injustice. He kept speaking out against persecution and against those who advocated the acceptance of segregation.

On February 20, 1895, Douglass left Cedar Hill to attend a women's rights meeting. Back home for an early supper, he and his wife were waiting for a carriage to take them to a meeting in a neighborhood church when suddenly he fell to the floor and died. His body was taken to Rochester, where he was buried in Mount Hope Cemetery, near his first wife, Anna, and their daughter Annie.

Now there are many memorials to Frederick Douglass—statues raised in his honor, streets, schools, libraries, housing projects named for him, a museum dedicated to his work. But the greatest of all memorials is found in his own words. His ideas, his understanding, his passion, his actions all inspire everyone who seeks justice in this imperfect world.

BIOGRAPHICAL PROFILES AND PORTRAITS

Susan Brownell Anthony

Anthony Burns

Anna Murray Douglass

Abby Kelley Foster

William Lloyd Garrison

Wendell Phillips

Charles Sumner

Toussaint L'Ouverture

Harriet Tubman

Ida B. Wells-Barnett

SUSAN BROWNELL ANTHONY
(1820–1906)

SUSAN B. ANTHONY FIRST MET FREDERICK DOUGLASS WHEN she was managing her family's farm near Rochester, New York. Douglass had chosen the city as the site for his newspaper, the *North Star*, because it had a very supportive Female Anti-Slavery Society. A frequent guest in her home, he fired her interest in reforms, including woman's rights and abolition.

She was a superb organizer and a prime mover in the woman's rights movement. Committed also to antislavery, she often risked the violence of hostile mobs. During the Civil War she rallied popular support for black emancipation. Douglass worked for both woman's suffrage and black suffrage as the foundation for Reconstruction.

But when Douglass gave priority to black suffrage, saying that while the ballot was desirable to women, to blacks it was a matter of life and death, Anthony and her allies felt betrayed. Later she and Douglass reconciled. Anthony continued to speak out strongly against lynchings, race riots, and discrimination of any kind. She headed the National American Suffrage Association from 1892 to 1900. She died at age eighty-six.

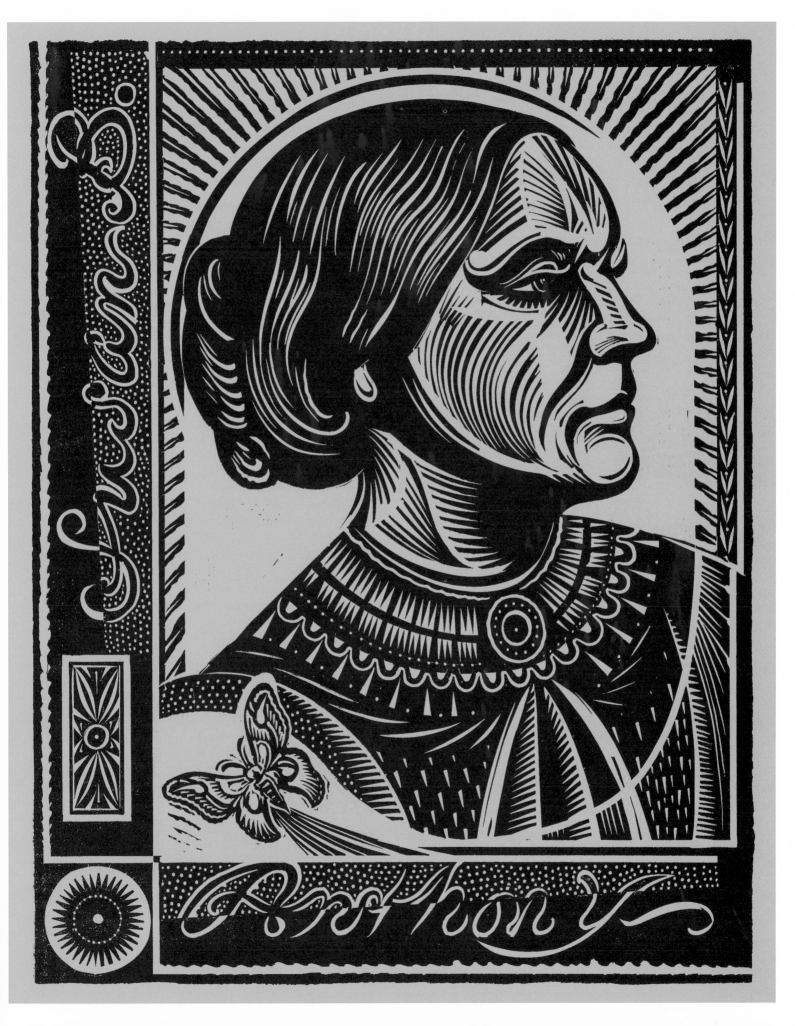

Anthony Burns
(1834–1862)

ANTHONY BURNS WAS AT THE CENTER OF THE MOST FAmous fugitive slave case in the pre–Civil War era. He was born a slave in Virginia, and early on defied law by learning to read and write. Converted to the Baptist faith while a young man, he began to preach. When his owner hired him out, he gained enough autonomy to plan his escape. In February 1854, at the age of nineteen, he hid himself on a ship bound from Richmond to Boston, where he found work. Ironically his ability to write led to his capture. A letter home was intercepted; it revealed where he was, and his master demanded that the Boston court return him to slavery in accord with the Fugitive Slave Law. Despite the frantic mobilization of the abolitionists to save him, government forces succeeded in shipping Burns back to Virginia in June 1854.

The Burns case occurred at a time of intense public turmoil over slavery and its extension into the territories. The mass attempt to rescue Burns helped crystallize Northern opposition to slavery and made thousands even more determined to resist the law. It was the last time a runaway slave was removed from Boston. Burns later was purchased by another owner, who freed him when several Bostonians, black and white, raised the necessary funds. Burns enrolled at Oberlin College and then became minister of a small Baptist church in Canada. He died there in 1862.

ANNA MURRAY DOUGLASS
(CA. 1813–1882)

ANNA MURRAY WAS BORN ON THE EASTERN SHORE OF Maryland probably five years before Douglass. Her parents were slaves, freed only a month prior to Anna's birth. At seventeen she began domestic service, working for various families in Baltimore over the years. There she met the young Frederick. They fell in love and planned to marry when he would be free. As soon as he escaped and reached the North, Anna joined him. They were married in 1838.

She worked as a household servant in New Bedford, Massachusetts, while she and Frederick struggled to establish a family. They had five children—three boys and two girls. But Douglass's commitment to abolition, his ceaseless lecture tours, and intense work as editor left him little time for domestic life. It is hard to know Anna's feelings about his frequent and often prolonged absences for she was illiterate the whole of her life; she wrote no letters and kept no diary.

They moved to Lynn, and six years later, in 1847, to Rochester, New York. During Frederick's two years in Great Britain, Anna had stayed at home with the children. When the Civil War came, two of their sons served with the Massachusetts Fifty-fourth Regiment. In 1872 the Douglass home in Rochester was destroyed by fire, and the family moved to Washington, D.C. In 1878 Douglass bought a fifteen-acre estate with a twenty-room house, "Cedar Hill," in Anacostia, D.C.

Anna Douglass died on August 4, 1882. She was about sixty-nine. She and Douglass had been married forty-four years.

ABBY KELLEY FOSTER
(1811–1887)

THE RADICAL ABOLITIONIST AND FEMINIST ABBY KELLEY Foster was much admired by Douglass, who often toured the abolitionist lecture circuit with her. In doing so Abby broke a strict taboo against traveling with a man, and a black man at that. Sometimes when she spoke at a meeting held in a church, the minister, shocked by a woman taking to the public platform, would order everyone out of the building. She made hundreds of speeches for the American Anti-Slavery Society and was also a militant advocate of women's rights.

Born in Massachusetts to a Quaker farm family, she was the seventh daughter in a time when farmers prayed for boys. She was raised in the town of Worcester, completed grammar school, and was one of the rare girls to go on to higher education, at a Quaker school in Providence, Rhode Island. She alternated studying with spells of teaching children to earn her way.

Hearing a lecture on slavery by William Lloyd Garrison changed the course of her life. While teaching in Lynn, Massachusetts, she joined the local female antislavery society and soon became a paid lecturer for the abolition movement. In 1838 Douglass wrote to tell her of "my respect and gratitude to you, for having stood forth so nobly in defense of woman and the slave. . . . It rejoices my soul to meet with an abolitionist who has turned her back on prejudice."

She married Stephen S. Foster, a "radical of radicals," in 1845, and they often traveled together as abolitionist speakers. They had one daughter, Pauline. They worked their farm in Worcester and made it a haven for fugitive slaves.

Abby Kelley

WILLIAM LLOYD GARRISON
(1805–1879)

THE FIRST TIME DOUGLASS HEARD GARRISON SPEAK WAS before an integrated audience in New Bedford, Massachusetts, where the young fugitive slave had recently settled. Garrison's passionate denunciation of slavery was a voice Douglass would never forget. Listening to it, he decided that he too would become an orator, speaking out against the evil of slavery no one knew more intimately. The two men became co-workers in the cause and fast friends. They had strong differences over policy at times, with bitter words exchanged, but Douglass remained loyal to his mentor to whom he felt deeply indebted.

Garrison was born in Newburyport, Massachusetts. He had only brief schooling before being apprenticed at thirteen to a newspaper editor. After working on local papers, he moved to Boston at age twenty-three to edit a reform journal. He was jailed briefly at one time on the charge of libel. On January 1, 1831, he founded the *Liberator* to launch his crusade against slavery. He ran the paper for thirty-five years, demanding immediate and unconditional emancipation. He helped form the American Anti-Slavery Society in 1833. He opposed Douglass when Douglass founded his own newspaper, the *North Star,* and was angered when Douglass went beyond moral opposition to slavery and advocated political action. After the Civil War, Garrison joined other reform movements, including temperance and women's suffrage.

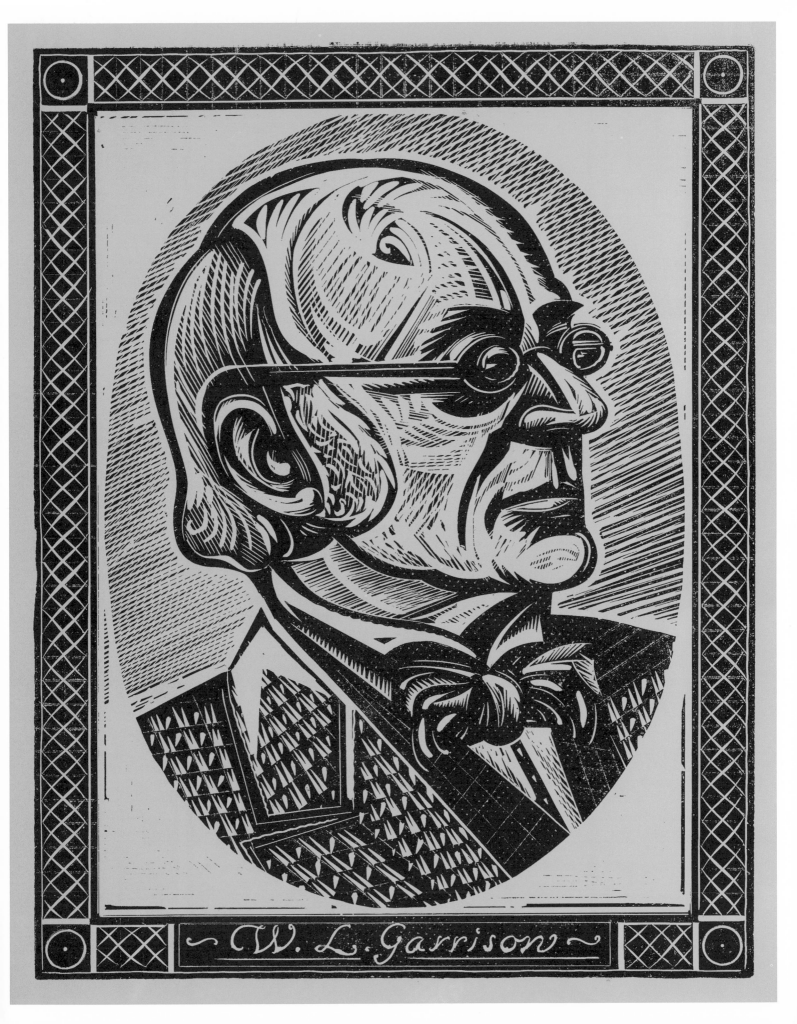

~ W. L. Garrison ~

Wendell Phillips
(1811–1884)

Wendell Phillips was one of the most outstanding white abolitionists. With William Lloyd Garrison, he drew Douglass into the antislavery organization, encouraging the young fugitive slave to tell his story to audiences and signing him up as a lecturer for the American Anti-Slavery Society. When *A Narrative of the Life of Frederick Douglass, An American Slave* appeared in 1845, the book opened with a preface by Garrison and a letter to Douglass from Phillips, meant to authenticate the brilliant memoir by a man so recently escaped from slavery. Phillips wrote of how "endeared you are to so many warm hearts by rare gifts, and a still rarer devotion of them to the service of others."

Phillips, a Boston aristocrat, was a Harvard graduate trained as a lawyer. Reading, in 1833, *An Appeal for That Class of Americans Called African* by Lydia Maria Child, "obliged me to come out as an abolitionist," he said. His oratorical powers helped recruit many men and women to the abolitionist cause. He was a frequent contributor to Garrison's *Liberator* who opposed the annexation of Texas, the Mexican War, and the Compromise of 1850. In the Civil War, he mustered pressure upon Lincoln to move toward emancipation. His humanitarian concerns extended to other causes: abolition of capital punishment, votes for women, the rights of labor, and reform of Indian policy. He was ranked with Douglass as one of the greatest orators of his time.

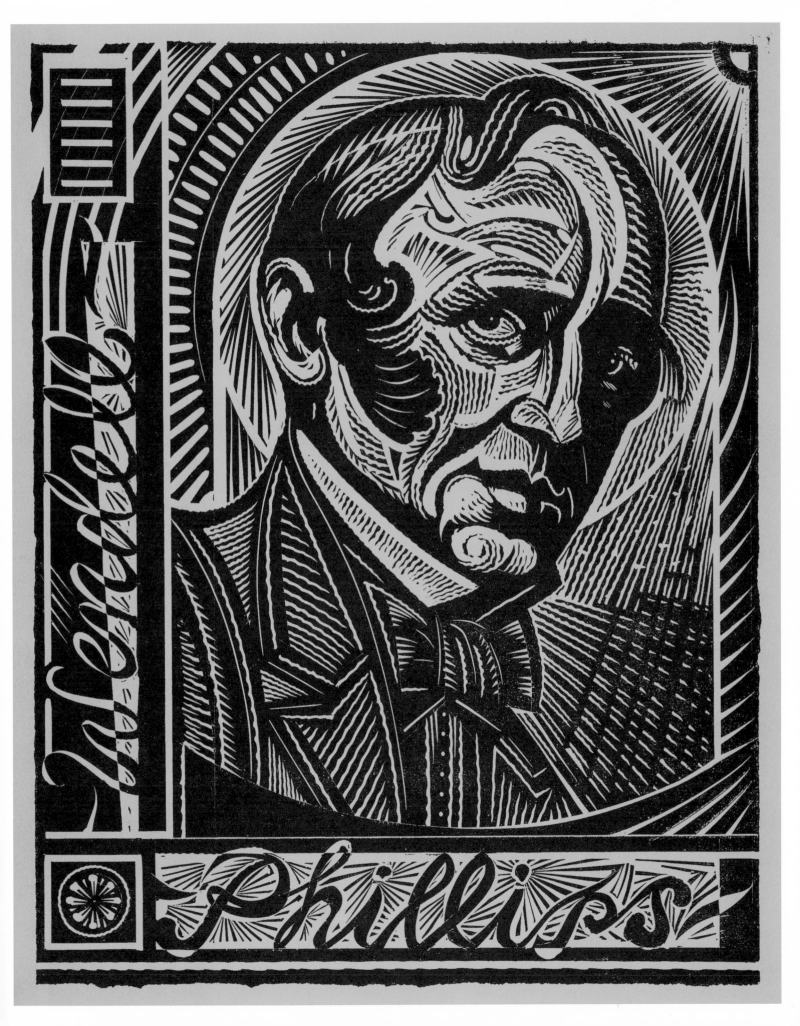

CHARLES SUMNER
(1811–1874)

ONE OF THE MOST DISTINGUISHED SENATORS OF THE nineteenth century was Charles Sumner of Massachusetts. An ardent abolitionist, his powerful speeches won the admiration of Douglass. Born in Boston, Sumner graduated from Harvard College and Harvard Law School. Sumner opposed the Mexican War, helped found the Free Soil Party in 1848, and as its candidate won a Senate seat in 1851. Thereafter he was reelected on the Republican ticket three times, serving until his death.

Sumner spoke out passionately against slavery, attacked the Fugitive Slave Bill of 1850, and opposed the Kansas-Nebraska Act of 1854. In his "Crime against Kansas" speech in May 1856, he attacked Southern efforts to extend slavery into Kansas and criticized Senator Andrew P. Butler of South Carolina. Shortly after, Butler's cousin, Congressman Preston Brooks, brutally caned Sumner at his Senate seat, forcing Sumner's absence from the Senate for over three years while he recovered.

Early in the Civil War, Sumner pressed Lincoln for emancipation and helped design the plan for Radical Reconstruction. He championed equal voting rights for blacks and whites. Douglass considered him one of the most dependable allies of African-Americans. Although Douglass differed with Sumner over the Senator's opposition to expansion overseas by annexation, their disagreement did not end their friendship.

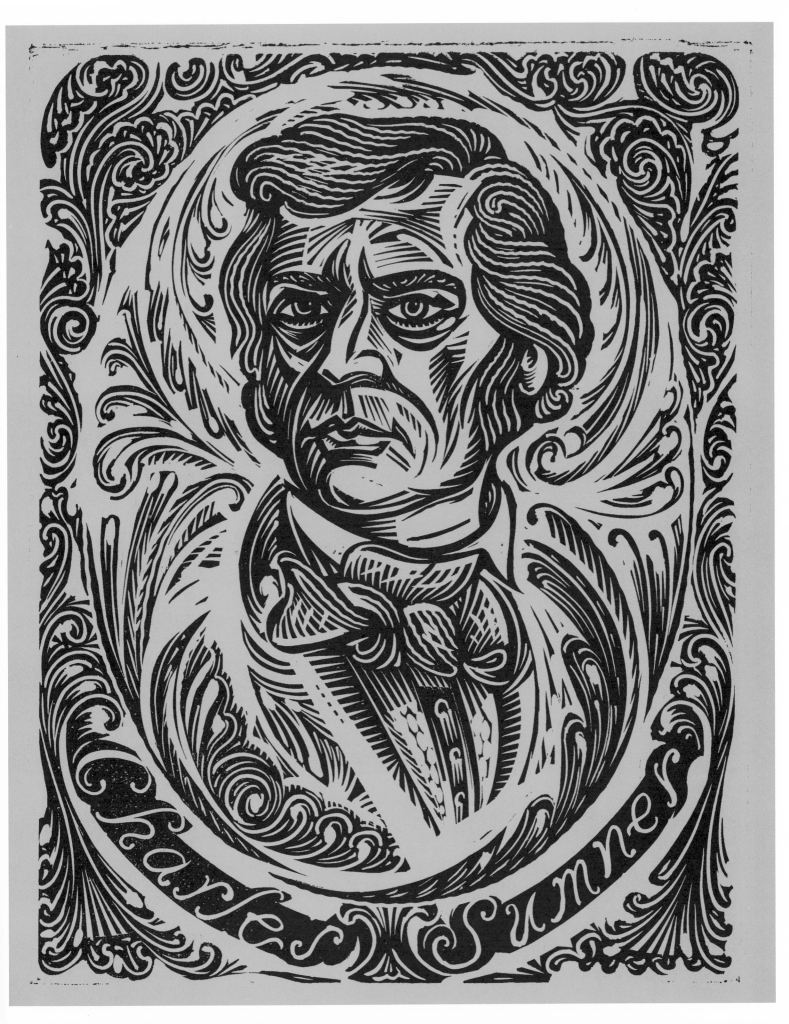

TOUSSAINT L'OUVERTURE
(CA. 1744–1803)

Toussaint L'Ouverture was the greatest of black heroes to Douglass. Haiti, the black republic Toussaint had wrested from slaveholders, was the only independent black nation in the Western Hemisphere. And along with Liberia and Ethiopia, it was one of only three in the world. Douglass served as U.S. Minister to Haiti in 1889–91, under appointment by President Harrison. And in 1892, Haiti appointed Douglass as the commissioner of the Republic's pavilion at the Chicago world's fair marking the four hundredth anniversary of Columbus's voyage to America.

Toussaint's father had been the son of a minor chieftain in Africa. Toussaint, the eldest of eight children, was captured in war and sold by slavers to a Haitian planter. The master encouraged Toussaint to read history, politics, and military science. He made him his coachman and then steward of his estates. During the French Revolution that began in 1789, Haiti's slaves, refused freedom by the French National Assembly, revolted. Toussaint, a gray-haired man of forty-five, organized the slaves into a revolutionary army that defeated the European troops. But when Napoleon made himself dictator of France, determined to destroy Toussaint and recover Haiti, he sent an expeditionary force to Haiti. Large-scale fighting with great loss of life followed, and Toussaint was forced to accept a peace offer. He quit public life and retired to his plantation. But the French kidnapped him and shipped him to France, where Napoleon flung him into a mountain dungeon. He died there on April 7, 1803. Seven months later, Napoleon gave up on his attempt to force Haiti back into slavery. The French withdrew and on the last day of 1803, Haiti formally proclaimed its independence.

HARRIET TUBMAN
(CA. 1820–1913)

LIKE DOUGLASS, HARRIET TUBMAN, THE DAUGHTER OF Benjamin and Harriet Ross, was born into slavery in Maryland. Her childhood was brutal—she was subject to heavy work as a field hand and frequent punishment by whipping. Once she was struck on the head with a rock by her master, a blow so violent it caused spells of unconsciousness for the rest of her life.

At about age twenty-five, Harriet escaped to the North. She became a remarkably resourceful and ingenious conductor on the underground railway, making nineteen trips back to the South to lead some three hundred people out of bondage. At one time rewards offered for her capture totaled $40,000.

During the Civil War, she served the Union forces as cook, scout, spy, and nurse. She made Auburn, New York, the permanent home for herself and her parents, and later converted her home into an old-age residence for indigent African-Americans.

Douglass saw her often over the years, and when a book about her was about to be published, he contributed an eloquent foreword. She was a suffragist and a founder of the National Association of Colored Women.

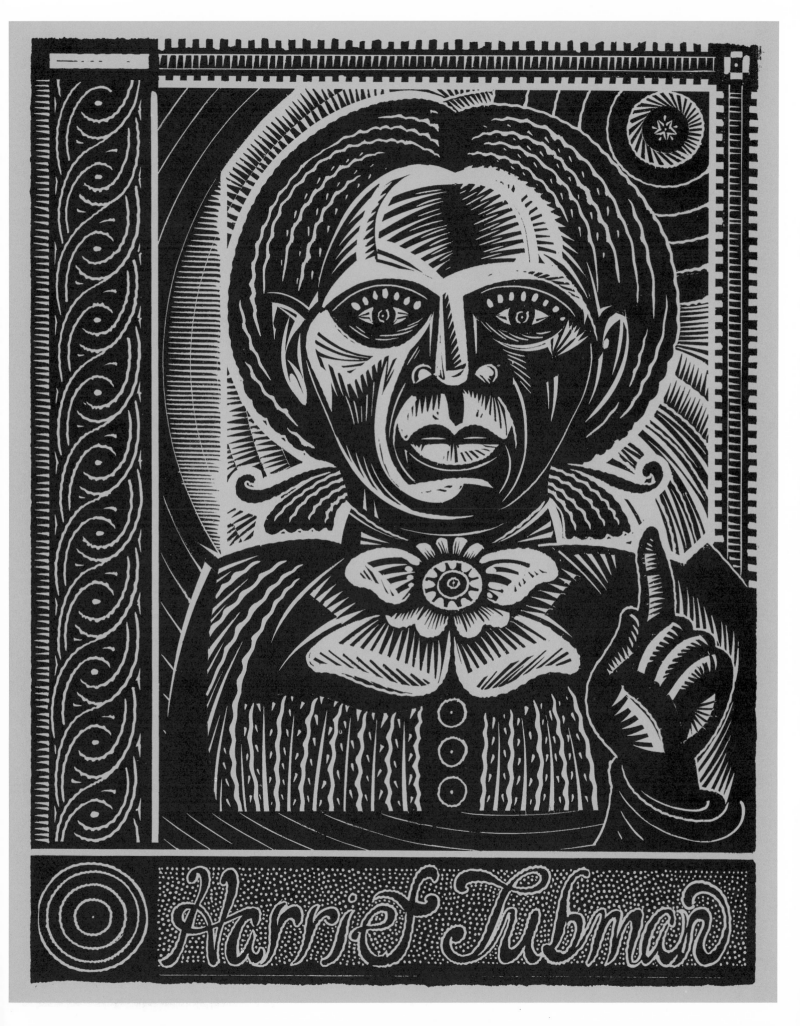

IDA B. WELLS-BARNETT
(1862–1931)

IN 1892, WHEN DOUGLASS WAS IN HIS SEVENTIES, HE CAME to call on the young writer and editor, Ida B. Wells. He wanted the uncompromising militant to know how indebted he was for her courageous exposure of lynchings. The old veteran of the struggle for freedom and equality generously acknowledged the brilliant contributions the thirty-year-old black journalist was making through her detailed investigations of the killings of African-Americans by white racist mobs.

Wells was born of slave parents in Holly Springs, Mississippi, in 1862. When freedom came, her mother worked as a cook and her father as a carpenter. Ida attended Rust University, a freedmen's high school in her hometown. She taught school there as well as in Tennessee, took classes at Fisk University, and began to contribute articles to the small black newspapers springing up.

In 1892 she became a full-time journalist on the *Memphis Free Speech*. When three men she knew were lynched that year, she denounced the crime in her paper, charging the murders had nothing to do with the old pretext of rape, but that the victims had been killed because they had been competing successfully with white storekeepers. Her newspaper office was wrecked and she was driven out of town. It launched her on a one-woman crusade against lynching. She lectured in the U.S. and abroad, founded antilynching societies and an organization to combat racial segregation. She married Ferdinand Barnett, a Chicago lawyer and editor who joined her crusade. In 1895 she published *A Red Record*, an account of three years' lynchings in the South. Douglass wrote the preface, one of his last acts, in the year of his death.

A NOTE ON SOURCES

WHAT FREDERICK DOUGLASS SAID OR WROTE WAS SO VOLUMINOUS AND SCATtered that there is as yet no complete collection of his words. The first scholarly attempt to gather the documents was made by Professor Philip Foner. Called *The Life and Works of Frederick Douglass* (New York: International), it was published in four volumes between 1950 and 1955 and supplemented by a fifth volume in 1975.

In the 1970s, with new sources becoming available, Professor John W. Blassingame and a team of editors began the monumental task of collecting and publishing a comprehensive edition called *The Frederick Douglass Papers* (New Haven: Yale University Press) to be issued over the years in three series. Series one: *Speeches, Debates and Interviews* appeared in five volumes. Yet to come are Series Two: *Published Writings*, and Series Three: *Letters*.

The complete texts of selections made for this book may be found in the scholarly editions of Foner or Blassingame. My own edition owes much to their scholarship.

DOUGLASS'S AUTOBIOGRAPHICAL WORKS

Narrative of the Life of Frederick Douglass, an American Slave, Written by Himself. Boston: Anti-Slavery Office, 1845. (Available now in several paperback reprints.)

My Bondage and My Freedom. New York: Miller, Orton & Mulligan, 1855.

Life and Times of Frederick Douglass, Written by Himself. Hartford, Conn.: Park Publishing, 1881.

Life and Times of Frederick Douglass, Written by Himself: His early life as a slave, his escape from bondage, and his complete history to the present time. New rev. ed. Boston: DeWolf, Fisk, & Co., 1892. Reprint, Collier, 1962.

BIOGRAPHIES OF FREDERICK DOUGLASS

Bontemps, Arna. *Free at Last: The Life of Frederick Douglass*. New York: Dodd, Mead, 1971

Foner, Philip. *Frederick Douglass: A Biography*. New York: International, 1964.

Huggins, Nathan I. *Slave and Citizen: The Life of Frederick Douglass*. Boston: Little, Brown, 1980.

McFeely, William S. *Frederick Douglass*. New York: W. W. Norton, 1991.

Preston, Dickson J. *Young Frederick Douglass: The Maryland Years*. Baltimore: Johns Hopkins University Press, 1980.

Quarles, Benjamin. *Frederick Douglass*. New York: Atheneum, 1968.

OTHER WRITINGS ON DOUGLASS

Readers who wish to examine critical estimates of the work of Douglass, or to learn more about the times in which he played so great a part, will find these books helpful:

Andrews, William L., ed. *Critical Essays on Frederick Douglass*. Boston: G. K. Hall, 1991.

Blight, David W. *Frederick Douglass' Civil War: Keeping Faith in Jubilee*. Baton Rouge: Louisiana State University Press, 1989.

Draper, Theodore. *The Rediscovery of Black Nationalism*. New York: Viking, 1970.

Foner, Eric. *Nothing But Freedom: Emancipation and Its Legacy*. Baton Rouge: Louisiana State University Press, 1983.

Foner, Philip, ed. *Frederick Douglass on Women's Rights*. New York: Da Capo, 1992.

Gates, Henry L., Jr., ed. *The Classic Slave Narratives*. New York: Penguin, 1987.

Katz, Jonathan. *Resistance at Christiana*. New York: Crowell, 1974.

Kousser, J. Morgan and James M. McPherson, ed. *Region, Race, and Reconstruction*. New York: Oxford, 1982.

McPherson, James M. *The Negro's Civil War*. New York: Ballantine, 1991.

Martin, Waldo E., Jr. *The Mind of Frederick Douglass*. Chapel Hill: University of North Carolina Press, 1984.

McGary, Howard and Bill E. Lawson. *Between Slavery and Freedom*. Bloomington: Indiana University Press, 1992.

Quarles, Benjamin. *The Negro in the Civil War*. Boston: Little Brown, 1953.

Ripley, Peter C., ed. *Witness for Freedom: African-American Voices on Race, Slavery, and Emancipation*. Chapel Hill: University of North Carolina Press, 1993.

Sterling, Dorothy. *The Trouble They've Seen: Black People Tell the Story of Reconstruction*. Garden City, New York: Doubleday, 1976.

Stuckey, Sterling. *Slave Culture*. New York: Oxford, 1987.

Sundquist, Eric J., ed. *Frederick Douglass: New Literary and Historical Essays*. New York: Cambridge University Press, 1990.

INDEX